750

Invisible Gardens

THOMAS DUNNE BOOKS *St. Martin's Press* ✹ *New York*

Invisible Gardens

Julie Shigekuni

This is a work of fiction. All characters and events
portrayed in this novel are either products of the
author's imagination or are used fictitiously.

THOMAS DUNNE BOOKS.
An imprint of St. Martin's Press.

www.stmartins.com

ISBN 0-312-31183-4

First Edition: June 2003

10 9 8 7 6 5 4 3 2 1

For Frances

The mind...should be like a river gorge with a swan flying overhead; the river has no desire to retain the swan, yet the swan's passage is traced by its shadow, without any omission.

LIN CHING-HSI

Invisible
Gardens

The same this year as last, the cranes fly down from Canada on their migration south, their destination in Texas still a long way off. They appear in the autumn sky as black specks over the Bosque, dirt on a lens of liquid blue. Set against the parched mountains, they could be insects swarming, except they are still miles off. Assuming shape as they approach, growing larger and more spectacular than anything I've ever seen, each bird is perfect, the mass a collage that moves the sky.

The silhouette of their long, thin necks and orbed bodies lingers like a storm front whose rain is destined to fall elsewhere. As they prepare to land in the marshland, their bony legs splayed and hanging, knees inverted over bloated bodies, they become at once awkward and preposterous.

A single coyote masquerades as a tourist on the shoreline, its presence unannounced and unrecognized by the birds as they feed, desperate to fill their bellies before moving on. A crane pulls its head from the shallow water, turns, opens its enormous wings like a yawn, the length of its neck crooked in the coyote's mouth.

Time stops as all eyes fasten on the bird. The mind cannot grasp what the eyes see. A sight so violent and so beautiful that it cannot be dismissed.

"Is it dead?" She hides her eyes behind cupped hands, a delayed response because the thing that frightens her has already passed. "That beautiful bird. Is it dead?"

"Fascinating," she thinks she hears the man next to her say. "Incredible." His voice is muffled, his back to her as he speaks into the tripod, scanning the scene and focusing the onocular lens.

"May I have a look?" she asks.

He moves aside so that she can take a turn at the lens, but there is nothing to see. The coyote is gone, disappeared along with the bird. The crane becomes invisible, like its predator. Feathers loft into the air and skim the water's surface before sinking into the mud.

One

It is inevitable. Her back pressed against the hardwood chair in the dull evening light, the dinner plates cleared from the table, the dishwasher churning a few feet away. Like the cup her baby held earlier in the day that seeped milk through an invisible crack, draining mysteriously between fingers, she feels her body emptying itself. Seated across from her husband, she clutches the rim of the old teak table, pulls air into her lungs, and holds it there, then lets what is inside disperse. She can hear Joseph calling her back, but suspended at an uncanny angle, she lingers, ignoring him. Her breath flows in and out of her body like a slippery tide, and she notes how peaceful it is to feel so light, so singular and removed. The noise her children make, even Joseph's voice, cannot reach her in this place she inhabits alone. Sound gathers in her ears like the warm and hollow beat of a drum; the thick red-browns of wood and brick floors bleed into a mass so huge it might contain the earth. She hears the distinct, familiar rhythm of Joseph's voice, but she's left the comfort of earth and home for a void that encircles her and cannot be silenced.

"Lily," Joseph calls again. "Are you with me?"

She is a ripe summer peach tumbling from a shelf, bruised and dumb, yet she can feel the soft damaged spot just under the skin, and she struggles to hide it from him. She knows she has entered the room without grace. Her eyes dart from one end to the other, as if sight itself might assure her that nothing has changed inside. Her children are okay, Joseph is there. *She* is okay. But across the room Joseph continues to stare. Next to him, two other sets of eyes, smaller ones, also stare. "Are you okay, Mommy?" Jessie pleads.

"I'm okay, really." Smiling, she rises from the chair, concentrating on putting one foot in front of the other as she makes her way down the hall.

"Come on, you two." She points over her shoulder at her children. "It's bath time."

L ater, in the quiet darkness of the bedroom she shares with Joseph, she complains that it's hard to keep up. When she moved west with her husband and their young daughter and younger son, the house they bought, though exactly what they had dreamed of, needed repair, and it has taken the summer and now into the fall to patch the roof, fix plumbing and electrical, clear out the yard that had been neglected when the house lay empty. Joseph hired a handyman to help with the repairs while he was away at work, and even though the man is gone now, finished with the work, Lily can still hear his footfalls on the roof and see him appearing around corners, through windows or open doors or on top of the roof to watch her pushing the baby on the swing and make conversation over Jessie splashing in the wading pool in the hot afternoons. She might have been grateful for some adult company, but she also considered Emilio's presence an intrusion on the life she shared with her children. Having just barely made their entrance into the world, they clung so close she often felt them as parts of her body; they thrived on touch, the baby lifting her shirt to suckle the breasts that he considered his, the older child turning circles in and out of Lily's legs. This was her private world that she shared only with them, and Emilio was large and unkempt, his round belly hanging over the waistband of his jeans.

Lily knew that her children sensed her aversion to Emilio; that their mother's apprehension, coupled with the stranger's unshaven face and untidy appearance and smell, frightened them. And perhaps because she sensed her children's fear, she struck up a friendly rapport with Emilio and encouraged Jessie and Misha to accept his presence with kindness. She made the children take turns filling a pitcher with water and ice so that he would not dehydrate in the hot New Mexico sun, and because she had never been comfortable giving orders, she replaced the water with beer on Friday afternoons and made polite, inquisitive conversation to pass the long days. She knew that Emilio found her attractive, that it was not her children he stopped to admire as much as the look of her in shorts wet from Jessie's splashing, her body in fluid motion as the breeze off the swing caught in her long black hair, laughing with delight as she tended to her children. She found nothing about Emilio attractive, but she flirted with him nonetheless. She imagined he would have fucked her crudely if given the opportunity, but she was well protected by her husband and surrounded every minute by her children and warm air and sunlight.

The morning Jessie let Emilio in for breakfast, Lily had been in the shower. It was just past eight, and Joseph had been called to autopsy only minutes before: bodies were being brought in from a rush-hour bus wreck on the interstate. Lily came down the hall in her white robe, hair slung up in a towel.

"Emilio," she called, pulling nervously on the sash of her robe, surprised to see him seated at the breakfast table, then noting from the stench that he'd been drinking. "When did you get here?"

"Emilio wants French toast, too," Jessie commanded, waving the tines of her empty fork through the air, reminding Lily of her promise to fix the children breakfast after her shower.

"I'll get to your French toast just as soon as I can." Lily looked from Jessie to Misha, uncomfortable that they had been alone in the house with a stranger, and one who'd been drinking at that.

Jessie, as if reading her mind, smiled, apparently unharmed. "I let Emilio in all by myself!"

"What a big girl you are. Only I've told you before that when Mommy is in the shower, you mustn't open the door. Haven't I told you that before? What if it wasn't Emilio?"

"I said, 'Who is it?' And he said, 'It's Emilio.' That's how I knew." Jessie's face beamed in the morning light.

"I see," Lily said, dismissing her daughter. Removing the wet towel from her head, she ran her fingers through her hair. "Would you like some coffee, Emilio?"

"In fact, I would." Emilio rubbed his eyes, then brought his hands down hard on his thighs. "Long night last night."

Inhaling his sour breath was turning Lily's stomach. "Well, I'll put it in a disposable cup so you can take it outside with you."

After she had poured the coffee and set it on the table, she noticed a foil packet in front of Emilio. "What's that?" she asked.

"Oh, I almost forgot. That's venison. Shot it myself last weekend, then smoked it, and I thought you might like to try some. It's real good."

"What's venison?" Jessie asked.

Lily was considering a response when Emilio cut in. "It's deer."

"Deer meat?" Jessie was always interested in the origins of the food being offered her. Pork was pig meat, beef was cow. Such literalness did not bother her; if anything, it enhanced the taste.

Lily paused to consider what Jessie would make of eating venison, then Emilio barked, "Deer. You know, like Bambi."

Lily watched Jessie's face, sure she would find her own horror there, perhaps even tears, but her daughter's expression did not change. "I see," she said, pausing inquisitively. "Can I try it?"

"Me, too." Misha's mouth popped open like a baby bird's.

"You sure can." Emilio smiled. "Both of you can."

A knife and fork were produced and slices of venison offered around the table. Despite her aversion to the strong smell and her mistrust of Emilio, Lily knew she couldn't refuse such a gift. Jessie and Misha, Emilio, and even Bambi appeared before her, awaiting her response as she put the dark meat on her tongue and chewed.

. . .

They'd been living in their new house less than a month when Loren's blond head appeared over the fence one hot afternoon, followed by the long shadow of a garden hose.

"Hey!" Misha, who, along with his sister, had been engrossed in digging a trench, thrust out his hands to catch fat droplets of water on his fingertips. "Rain," he cheered.

"That's not rain." Jessie, the weather expert, followed the spray up the wall that delineated the extent of Misha's universe. "Do I know you?" She cocked her head suspiciously at Loren.

"I know *you*." Loren grinned. "You're Jessie, and he's Misha." She pointed the hose first at Jessie, then back at Misha, causing a round of delighted shrieks to ring through the yard. "And you moved here from New York."

"That's our mother," Jessie said, pointing a red shovel across the yard at Lily, who reclined in the shade.

Lily rose from the lawn chair, stretched, and walked to the wall where Loren stood. "Loren knows that because she works at the hospital with Daddy," she explained to no one, for her children had gone back to their digging. To Loren, she confided, "I'm trying to wean my children of their distrust of strangers. It seems New Mexico's a lot friendlier than where we used to live."

Single and childless at thirty, Loren took an interest in Jessie and Misha, volunteering to watch them whenever Lily needed help. Lily reported on her conversations with Emilio in a tone of wry amusement, in ways that often made Loren laugh, though one weekend Emilio's childhood friend had, in a freak accident, been dragged behind a truck and wound up on Joseph's table in the morgue. Lily had comforted Emilio then, sat beside him listening as his sad eyes filled with grief. Lily told Loren about the venison and how, after serving it, Emilio had gone outside to collect tumbleweeds and debris and set them in pyres around the yard, which had upset her. Fires scared her, even when they were controlled burns, and she worried over the lizards that had made their habitat under stacks of dead branches, the warty toads that would seize up in your palm as if turning to stone. Her husband had captured one between his hands and brought it inside to let Jessie and Misha finger its tough, bumpy skin; and Lily's dogs chased the toads, as well as the rabbits that slipped through the wood-slatted fence early every morning to eat grass and steal vegetables from the garden.

She remembers the day the dark clouds gathered to the east, signaling the arrival of the first afternoon storm of the monsoon season. She and Loren were seated side by side at the redwood picnic table, drinking sun tea under the portico, monitoring the thunderheads over the Sandias with one eye, the children with the other.

"In two minutes you and Misha need to get out of the pool," Lily finally announced to her daughter. "A storm's coming in."

Jessie, pretending not to hear the warning, slipped under the surface of the water and came up, seal-like and sputtering, with an announcement of her own. "I'm learning to swim!"

"Two minutes," Lily called again, and then, surveying the yard and all that had been made hers through hard work and patient nurturing, she said to Loren, "You know, I don't mean to sound boastful, but at this minute I think I have the perfect life."

I t's pretty here, isn't it?" she says to Joseph in the darkness. She is stating a fact, but she poses it as a question because she wants to hear his voice once more before she falls asleep.

She can hear his breath lengthening beside her and has almost given up on a response when he says back, "Huh?"

"Our house, our life. The move. It turned out good, don't you think?"

Joseph shifts on his pillows and, turning to face his wife, strokes her hair. "Yes, sweetheart." How like Joseph to sound both exasperated and willing to indulge her. "What's wrong?"

"Nothing," she says.

"Good," he sighs, smacking his lips together as if to taste how good it is.

"We're lucky, aren't we?" This time her questioning tone is unintentional.

"I'm lucky to have you." She can hear the smile in his voice. Then, throwing his leg over hers, he begins almost instantly to snore.

"Hey." She pulls her leg out from under his.

"What?" He rolls away, irritated now.

She taps him on the shoulder to call him back. "I'm okay now," she says.

"Good," he says.

"I wanted you to know that," she declares. "In case you were worried. I've just been caught up. That's all."

"I won't worry." He turns back to face her, now fully awake. "I guess I've been caught up, too."

"Yes." She cannot say for sure what she is agreeing to, but she thinks how strange it is that Joseph's job as a pathologist is to normalize tragedy. How can he stand each morning to carve open bodies from which all essence of life has departed, to mutilate and eviscerate what is inside, creating a cadaver that can be sewn back together and viewed as if it were alive? It's creepy, she thinks. Yet she has come to see her husband's daily work as symbolic of what he has done for her, and she is grateful for the life she would not have without him. She thinks of him as a large, unsinkable vessel, remembers how he came to her brimming and abundantly full. His eyes reflect the blue of sky and waves. She sees him as if from above, glimpses in his eyes what is dazzling and at once so solid and reliable that she cannot resist smiling. She holds his gaze for a moment, and he reads the signal well. Too well. Though sex was not what she had in mind, her body has spent years molding to his and has its own natural way of responding.

"I'm going to sleep." Her husband turns away from her afterward, his body satisfied. "Another long day tomorrow."

The sex should help her sleep, too, but it doesn't. Instead she stares out the open window at the desert landscape, and she wonders how it is that she worked her whole life to wind up in this place where the ground appears frosted in the moonlight even though it isn't the least bit cold. But it's not really the desert she's thinking about. Her job at the university, the dissertation she rewrote into a book, now published. She's worked hard, attained the goals she had for most of her adult life, maybe longer. She's thirty-five, and every dream she's had up to now has come true. Including the children. She always knew she'd have two. In her mind, she can see their sleeping faces as clearly as Joseph's body beside her. Still, sleep does not come. Misha will wake up with the sun, she knows, and tomorrow she will be tired.

"So what's to be done with this perfect life?" she whispers, knowing that Joseph won't hear her now. She stares out the open window at the strange nighttime scenery, wondering what more there could possibly be to hope for.

The next day she has planned lunch with an important colleague, Perish Ishida. He's a high-ranking member in the tightly stratified department she's entering, but that's not why she's apprehensive about the lunch. There weren't many Japanese-Americans where she grew up in upstate New York; the ones she knew were relatives, or friends of relatives, and she believed she pretty much knew them all. But here in New Mexico, where the non-Anglos seem to be either Hispanic or Native American, she feels uneasy about having to share the department with someone named Perish Ishida. Applying lipstick in her compact mirror beforehand, she wonders if people will connect her hire to Perish. Or, worse yet, to the department needing one more Japanese-American to fill some secret quota. Maybe he's related to Ruy Ishida at the university where her father taught; perhaps

Ruy has been instrumental in bringing her on. She notes puffiness beneath her eyes and regrets not having slept better. She contemplates canceling and going home for a nap, guesses it will be difficult to concentrate on conversation, but she is wrong.

To her surprise, Perish Ishida is an engaging lunch companion.

"I come from California," he tells her once drinks have been served and they begin the wait for their entrees. Lily associates California with her mother, who's from there. "I'm one of a dozen children, and I spent my childhood in a one-bedroom house and outside in the woods."

Lily's own mother was from a big family and grew up poor. It isn't something Lily would have guessed about Perish, whose facial gestures and elegant hands strike her as refined. But now that he's said it, a picture takes shape in her mind while he talks. She imagines her mother—who has been dead for a decade—in the house that let the air travel freely through rotting slats of wood. A barefoot child crossing a floor of upturned, splintered wood, playing with rocks and string for toys.

She has always regretted that poverty is not something Joseph understands better. Not that he should have had to suffer, but this void in his experience both attracts and repels her. Joseph understands, instead of hunger, the benefits of a nourishing, slightly extravagant meal. He cooks her salmon on Saturdays, rib eye on Sundays, and supplies her with foolproof recipes tested by his mother for the weeknights when he is too busy to cook. Though she herself has never gone hungry, she believes that hunger is born into the bones. It's something she inherited from her mother, the same way Joseph inherited satiety from his. But more recently, she knows, Joseph has taught her how it feels not to be desperate, a thing she hadn't known until she met him. He's taught her about kindness and given her enough of it that she has something left over—first for their two small children, then for her students.

Thinking about her husband, she suddenly realizes that she's smiling, and that across the table, Perish is smiling back. His brown eyes glint in the sunlight, and she hesitates, wondering whether she should acknowledge that she has no idea what he's been talking about. She reaches across the table to touch his arm with her fingertips, meaning to apologize for her lack of attentiveness. But then she withdraws her hand. She doesn't know him well enough for that. "I'm sorry"—she squints across the table— "what were you saying?"

"Nothing." He's no longer smiling. Frown lines gather around his mouth, making him look older, embittered, and she wonders what he looked like twenty, or even ten, years ago. Wonders if she would have found him handsome then. "You were somewhere else entirely, weren't you."

"Yes," she admits, deciding he was probably never handsome. "I'm sorry."

"I'll forgive you," he says, "if you tell me what you were thinking."

"I was just thinking about my life," she says.

"What about your life?"

"What would you like to know?"

"Nothing." He smiles. "Everything."

Perish is a spectral presence, she decides as he talks. He's not

attractive, but he reflects parts of her life back to her in ways that
flatter her, and she's suddenly overcome with a rush of joy that
she can't quite account for. Sitting across from him, her hands
tucked tightly under her thighs, she can feel the heat of her body
in her fingertips. Later that same afternoon, he sends her a note
asking for a second lunch. She reads it in the mail room, her feet
shifting beneath her, and notes how his signature seems to dance
across the page.

It's October when Yas arrives. He comes to them by air, flown in
like fragile cargo, arriving damaged but unbroken. At the airport he shuffles down the tarmac past Lily and her children with
an absence that is both ominous and familiar. She has known for
years that there's something wrong with him, but she doesn't
identify the problem exactly until she's forced to chase him down.
She has not seen her father since her mother's funeral ten years
back, and since then the problem has come to her only in
hunches, gaps she sensed in their telephone conversations. It was
she who, in a moment of wanting to hold tight to what she felt
slipping away, invited him into her home. Now, with Misha in one
arm and Jessie in tow, she looks into his face, and tears come to
her eyes. Once a well-respected botanist, he can no longer hold a
job, and it isn't hard to see why. At the sight of her children, his
expression remains fixed and slightly bemused, as if he is looking
past them to a memory so distant it cannot be articulated.

"Is this Grandpa Yas?" Jessie demands in her childlike voice.

"Yes." Lily has tried to explain to Jessie about her grandfather, but the girl knows him only through stories. He is the man who studies flowers and trees and plants, believing that they contain within their powerful beauty the miracle of life. Once, when she was seven, Lily told Jessie, her cat Jupiter chewed the petal off a poisonous hybrid her father kept high on his study shelf. Jupiter with the silken fur who slept curled at Lily's head, purring in her dreams when she reached an arm up to stroke his plush belly. Who returned to Lily's bed to die in a pool of feces and vomit containing a soft red petal so toxic that even stomach acids had failed to break it down.

Though she did not tell Jessie this, Lily remembered the curve of her father's back as he peered through bifocals at Jupiter. The sharp tweezers that he pulled from his back pocket to extract a mass of red from the frothy bile that clung to Jupiter's mouth. The way his back straightened when he'd gotten what he was looking for, his stillness as he held the specimen above his head for closer inspection. He'd squinted into the light. "Extraordinary."

"Lily," her mother had called to her from the doorway. "He must have come to say good-bye."

"There could be no other explanation," her father concurred. "Normally, a cat would have wandered off."

Standing over Jupiter's slack body, Lily willed her cat to move, to purr like he had the night before when she'd woken, as she often did, to feel him above her head. In a dream, she'd fallen from the sky, dropped like a penny through miles of clouds, until she faced the ground directly beneath her. She'd had this dream of falling more than once, and that night as on all the other nights, she'd reached up to let Jupiter's plush warmth coax her back to sleep. Though she was not thinking of the dream, she knew she would not return to sleep in her bed alone.

Close by, her parents continued to converse in a cryptic hum of science and silence until her mother suggested she help her father dig a hole under the sycamore that brimmed over the far wall of the yard.

"I guess that's why you should never go near anything your father grows, at least without first knowing what it is," her mother cautioned, and as a display of sympathy, she let Lily sleep that night on a cot at the foot of her parents' bed.

African Queen, White Dragon, Ghurka, Immaculata, Princess Marina, delphinium. Lily knew the secret names her father gave his favorite flowers, and from age seven, she knew also that her father could not be trusted. Now, Lily understands, her daughter is being introduced to family secrets and the importance of names. Jessie listened when Joseph and Lily argued over whether her baby brother should be a Quinn like her and Joseph, or a Soto like Lily; would he take a Japanese first name or an American one? Lily's favorite author had been Yukio Mishima, but she hadn't liked the name Yukio, so Yukio Mishima became Misha Quinn. And there they were.

"Grandpa Yas?" Jessie calls softly into the rumble of footsteps and greetings that echo through the open space, and out of nowhere, Yas looks down at her and smiles.

In some ways, Yas has changed dramatically from the father Lily remembers, but his thoughts still seem to revolve around plants and trees and flowers. At breakfast the next morning, he points a bent finger out the window into the crisp fall air at an old elm that stands against the back fence amid the roses. "You don't need that one," he announces, glaring at it over his coffee cup. "It blocks the view of the mountains."

"I like that tree." Joseph glances up from the morning paper, following Yas's gaze out the window. "It's barren now, but I like its shape, and I like where it stands. It's one of the reasons we bought this house."

"It's not a good tree."

"It's a perfectly good tree."

Yas drops the subject then, slyly, till Joseph goes off to work; then Lily sees him from her bedroom window. She's wrapped in a bath towel when she spies him traipsing across the backyard with a ladder under his arm. His eyes are shielded by a baseball cap, as if in not being able to see her he might not be seen by her, and he carries in the other hand a saw.

By the time she gets dressed and out back, he is standing on the highest rung of the ladder with his arms outstretched as he hacks at a thick branch. "You can't do this," she protests, knowing that words are all she has to stop him. "Joseph will be furious."

"Can't you see?" he bellows. "This tree is shading the rose-bushes. Roses need at least ten hours of sunlight a day."

The first branch falls beside her with a dull thud. Glaring up at him, she wants to shake the ladder, imagines him tumbling to a violent death. His insolence is maddening, and the tree, the culprit, looks as sad and bald as the head of an old man. A month before, it shed its leaves; now it stands naked, as if ashamed of its crime.

. . .

L ily calls Joseph at the morgue to complain to him about her
father and what he's done, but Joseph is too busy to hear
her. It isn't until he arrives home and sits down to dinner that his
eye catches on the empty space that earlier in the day had held a
tree. Lily sees the anger register in her husband's face, notes it
rising as the children laugh along with Yas's jokes. They laugh
heartily and too loud, and Lily knows that this fake laughter irritates Joseph.

He addresses his anger to Lily. "Could you do something,
please?"

"Jessie, Misha," Lily calls softly to quiet them, "you're using
bad manners. Please try to behave at the table."

"But Grandpa Yas—" Jessie begins.

"Let's try not to pattern our behavior after Grandpa Yas,"
Joseph cuts in.

Lily finds Joseph's impatience disrespectful, but she doesn't say
anything. How can he not be troubled by the man who stares
blankly at her from across the dinner table and laughs flatly at
jokes no one gets? The mockery that once permeated his laughter
is gone, replaced by a hollowness that tells her he's forgotten what
he's laughing about. Perhaps because his mind has deteriorated, he
exists in a state of constant excitation where everything is the thing
in between and all things are interchangeable.

Yas's prattling continues, along with the children's laughter,
until Joseph explodes. "This is insanity," he bellows, as if the children and her demented father cannot hear.

The children gaze beseechingly at Lily; Yas stares at the rice and vegetables piled on his plate as if unable to make a connection between food and hunger. "Can we talk about it later?" Lily begs Joseph. "Not now, okay?"

"I can't deal with this," Joseph fumes between clenched teeth. "Someone's got to make him stop."

"I'm sorry," she says with quiet consternation. "I thought maybe you could talk to him, because he wouldn't listen to me."

"Fine." Joseph glances around the table, recognizing the level of upset he's caused with his temper. He makes a general statement: "Don't look at *me*." Then to Lily, "I know it's not your fault. I'll take care of it."

And to Jessie and Misha, "I'm going to plant a new tree this weekend. How does that sound?" He has managed to recover the proper paternal tenor. "You two want to help me?"

"You seem distant," Joseph proclaims that night, after the children and Yas have gone to bed.

Lily guesses this is her husband's way of calling her back, and she accepts it as that. "I'm fine." She smiles, though she feels more like crying.

She looks around the room at the sloping adobe walls, admiring them for their thickness, their ability to shut out sound and heat and cold and uphold a home that belongs to her but does not feel close.

She remembers the first night she spent with her husband. There in the loft in Larchmont that he had rented with his best friend from medical school. The slatted wood floors, stained a gray shade of blue that will always remind her of dreary New York skies. The threadbare mustard-colored sofa where they ate Chinese food, the cartons littered across the overcast floor. He sank back into the couch, and straddling him, she lay her head on his chest. "I can feel your heart beating," she said.

She had wanted him then, flirted with the idea of what it would feel like to let him inside her, but he was scared. "What does it sound like?" he asked, putting her off. "I don't think I've ever heard my own heart."

"It's strong and steady," she told him, "a good one, I think."

Later he told her that he knew they were entering into a lifetime that first night, and apologized for his unwillingness to make love to her by telling her how important it was to get the beginning right. Now she tries to find her way back there.

She has a slender, athletic body, but it's aging. Ten years ago, before the children, her wardrobe was T-shirts and jeans, no makeup, a deceptive move, a pretense, as if there were nothing to hide. As if blood and nerves did not keep time beneath the smooth, flat surface of her face. She kept her black hair long, parted at the side and tucked behind one ear. She was beautiful and she knew it, beautiful because she knew it. Joseph knew it. Her body defied him to think otherwise; urged him to feel, to want, to act on what he wanted. And when they made love, she could feel him pushing inside her, exploring the intricate landscape that lay hidden beneath her skin, like the moon that rose up when he held her in the dark.

"I love you like this." He had spoken into the shadows on the second floor of his loft, with its waist-high rectangular windows that showed only the branches of trees and houses below. "When your face opens up and I can tell what you're thinking."

He mistook craving for desire, hunger for longing, and set about filling the empty places in her heart, and she was touched by a love so profound it made her weep.

"Tell me what makes you sad," he asked afterward, when they were lying side by side with only their legs touching. They were staring at patterns of leaves projected on the ceiling, movement over a static backdrop.

"I don't know." She closed her eyes. "Do you ever feel loneliest when you're the least alone?"

"No," he said. "Lying here with you, I feel completely satisfied. And not at all lonely."

"My mother died five years ago," she told him after a while, when she'd opened her eyes again. "The year I graduated from college."

"I'm sorry," he said.

"Don't be," she said, because she knew he couldn't understand what she didn't yet understand herself, a loss that would come like waves sweeping her out to a place she'd never been, where everything was movement and the sting of salt made her tread with her eyes shut. "She was the person who loved me most in the world."

"You're so beautiful." Joseph's lips traced the arch of her eyebrows, the bridge of her nose.

Lily inhaled deeply and held the scent of him in her lungs. "I don't talk about my mother. I haven't talked to anyone about her since she died."

"Why not?"

Lily shrugged. "There really isn't a language to talk about what I lost when my mother died. It's as if there's nothing to say."

Joseph made the loss explicit, and made clear, too, that what was lost could never be regained. He cradled her against his chest, wrapped her in his freckled arms, and rocked her into sleep, promising her the safety of his body, someday the laughter of children, and life on an island so remote that despair might never find her there. They would take a day trip, skim across the surface of a sea so peaceful that waves lapped but did not rise up; sunlight and mild weather would pass into a gentle night. There was never a question but that they would arrive safely, and then, collecting materials that the tide had washed ashore, they would build a house that, in the middle of the desert, could not be penetrated by the sea. There, on the land, she would not think of her mother.

And so life went with Joseph, and the house was built and filled with children and now her father, too.

Since her mother's death, the image Lily sees of her is framed by the entryway to her parents' house in Oswego. She figures it must have been her first semester away at college—winter break, because the ground was thick with snow. She'd been surprised to find everything as it had been: her room freshly dusted by her mother, who kept the house meticulously ordered. In the bathroom, clean towels folded over the rack in thirds, an unused bar of soap, the countertops bare and ready for use. There was a logic to her mother's compulsion that defied the natural progression of time. It appeared in the windows, which were spotless and invisible, and in the white walls and white carpet and throw rugs that bore no sign of wear. The house might have lay uninhabited, except for the presence of her parents.

"*Itte kimasu,*" they always called to the house before leaving. Go and come back.

"*Itte irashai.*" I will leave and return.

"*Tadaima,*" Lily said reflexively when she entered the house that chilly late afternoon.

"*Okaeri ni.*" Her mother's voice rang out from the kitchen, and then she appeared in the entryway, looking not at all like the mother Lily remembered. In Lily's absence, age had entered the timeless perfection of her mother's face, and it struggled now to tell its story. Lily could not stop staring; neither could she shake the thought that these lines, like a map of routes that ran along her mother's eyes and mouth, marked somehow her own failing. Lily had never seen them before, yet perhaps they'd been there all along.

"You look good," Lily said, wanting to hear how such an observation might sound when uttered aloud. She stared from her father, whose smile seemed to be hiding something, to her mother, whose lips refused to part, and she found comfort in the same tight-lipped stoicism she had always known.

"You look good, too, *neh.*" Lily noted the slight tremor in her mother's voice. "But you mustn't become so *erai* that I don't recognize you anymore." Lily knew what this comment conveyed. Knowledge held in the mind meant betrayal to her mother. Standing in the entryway, Lily hesitated, her mind slipping outside to the greenhouse where her father kept his beloved plants.

His job entitled him to this dalliance, which his wife tolerated as long as the plants stayed out of the house. Lily remembered her father's attempts to drag certain favorites inside for show, the exotic species with their fancy Latin names. The pact between Lily and her mother was a simple and similar one: she could have her knowledge, but it must not enter the house, must not threaten their relationship, must not create a space between them. Still, how could she explain that it was not the books that had caused a change in her. Boys appeared everywhere, genuinely interested in how foreign she seemed, so remote, so beautiful. How could she say that she'd slept in a bed that was not her own. A heap of soiled covers on the floor, creating a gap that promised only to widen. There, in the entryway, something existed between Lily and her mother that had not been present before. They felt it in the air as something immutable and clear, and when Lily excused herself to her room, she wept violently into her pillow the tears that she could not summon later, at her mother's death.

So you said you'd tell me about your life," Perish begins the next time she sees him.

Lily is grading papers on the patio outside the campus coffee bar when he scoots a chair up beside her. She is flummoxed by his presence and speaks without thinking. "I have the perfect life," she says, but as soon as the words have left her lips, she wants to take them back. Perish sinks back in his seat, grinning, and she has the odd feeling that she's spoken about someone else's life, not hers.

"Look." He points into the clear blue sky where, in the distance, a yellow balloon is making its way up in the breeze. She sees the wavering yellow globe, and beneath it a looped red ribbon that perhaps connected it to a child's wrist. Now the string dangles in midair. "So do they call your husband Dr. Death?"

Lily focuses her attention on the man sitting across from her, stunned by his lack of sensitivity and by his prescience. It's not really the crude comment (being the wife of a pathologist, she's used to morbid humor), it's that indirectly—perhaps unwittingly—he's identified her sore spot. Since she arrived in New Mexico, she has often wondered if their department would have offered her a teaching post had Health Sciences not sought out Joseph. Perish has just made it clear that he knows about Joseph, the way every member of History most likely knows something of the details regarding her hire. "So what do *you* know about my husband?" Lily asks defensively.

"Just what I've heard, that he has a number of faculty falling over themselves—if doctors do that sort of thing."

"Yes, well, he *is* very good."

"But not as good as his wife."

Lily shifts in her seat. She guesses that Perish is only trying to flatter her, but she wishes he'd change the subject.

Perish cuts in to her thoughts. "I'm sorry. I can see that this is not turning into a good conversation. We don't have to talk about your husband."

"Thank you." Anxious for a distraction, Lily squints into the sky. She thinks she can still spot the yellow balloon, though the bright ribbon is no longer visible.

"Tell me about your family," he says. "Where do your parents live?"

Lily contemplates telling Perish that her mother is dead. But such a disclosure would lead to questions about an even more private subject.

"Another bad topic?" He smiles.

It's amazing to Lily how Perish somehow keeps pace with her shifting mood. As if he's taken a cue from her, he looks beyond her, his eyes widening. "My mother died when she was forty-nine. Not even fifty, my age now."

Forty-nine was the age of Lily's mother when she died. It's a remarkable coincidence, and one she chooses not to acknowledge. "I'm sorry," she says. "About your loss."

"Don't be sorry." Perish is still smiling.

The inside of a human body is like a flower," Joseph once told her. "When you pull the skin back and remove the chest plate, the colors there astonish you. Layers of fat that ripple like cream, organs that are purple and deep blue and scarlet."

Lily, who has never seen the inside of a body, imagined instead her father's garden with its exotic botanicals. The trumpeting pink amaryllis that he tended alongside pyracantha and hydrangea. But she knew she was way off.

"Doesn't it bother you?" she asked. "I mean, sticking your hands inside someone's body like that?"

"That's just it," he said. "The body belonged to a person, and that's what makes it intense. But the person is no longer alive. It's just a *body*. Most people don't want to think of it that way, but when you come face-to-face with death, it's less scary than you might imagine."

Lily has never been able to imagine how a corpse could be anything other than scary, but lately she has been thinking she might want to see one, and after chatting with Perish, she is filled with a sudden longing to visit the morgue where Joseph works.

When the buzzer outside the building signals her in, she pushes open the door to the medical investigators' office and remembers immediately why she has stayed away. The warm, insipid smell of rotting bodies and chemicals flows unmistakably through the air. The unpleasantness is offensive, and from behind the front desk, the receptionist's smile confuses her.

"I'm Joseph Quinn's wife, Lily." She wants to make the receptionist's smile go away, but it broadens at the mention of her name.

"Nice to meet you," the woman says. "What took you so long to find us?"

"It's nice to meet you, too." Lily extends her hand, ignoring the second statement, unwilling to consider that her absence has been conspicuous to everyone. Perhaps Joseph has mentioned her in his life here, so far from hers. Or perhaps he is in love with this woman. Lily doubts it, though the woman's fondness for Joseph is apparent.

"Joseph just got called to the autopsy suite, but I can page him for you if you'd like."

"No, that's okay." Lily is about to turn and leave, but the

receptionist smiles again and offers directions to the viewing room: down the long hall, second left, then a quick right. It feels like a bribe, but then that's why she's here. Lily senses how dangerous it might be not to follow these directions, perhaps even dangerous to follow them correctly. Down the hall, second left, quick right, and Lily is struck dumb by what she sees. Through a block of glass the size of a large television screen, an old man lies naked and still across a high chrome table. His skin is tinged gray, but somehow it manages to glow under the cold fluorescent light. The weight of his body sinks downward with a longing to return to the earth, and beneath him, blood collects in dark pools. The man's nipples are purple and stiff, as if frozen, though his penis lays flaccid and exposed, unashamed in death. Huddled around the man are the clinicians, indistinguishable in their blue scrubs. Lily does not recognize her husband among them at first. Then she spots him. The concentrated stare belongs without a doubt to Joseph; she can read his eyes even through the thick plastic goggles, the crease that forms like a bass clef along the smooth cheek she kissed good-bye that morning. She watches as he yanks the old man's skinny legs to break the rigor, and she imagines the strength such a maneuver must take, a kind of strength she does not possess. It does not occur to her to flinch or turn away from this act of violence. What she sees excites her, and she is unable to move.

Sound does not penetrate the glass, but she watches as Joseph signals instructions to the morphology technician and then stands back. The morph tech cuts a Y across the chest and down, then hacks through the ribs with a saw. A long, hollow needle is inserted into the open abdomen and fluid extracted, then measured. Lily at once understands the fascination on Joseph's face when he describes death to her. The terror and mystery that his stories evoke are all inside her as lengths of intestine are pulled from the man's lower abdomen, then a stomach, a liver, and a heart are lifted like so many rabbits from a magician's hat. She does not know how long she has been watching when Joseph sees her. Dropping his goggles to his chest, he tilts his head and peers through the clear glass, then lowers his mask and blows her a kiss.

She does not stay to watch the body being sutured shut. She is light-headed when she leaves the building and as she walks, the glare of the afternoon sun on her back, she realizes that she is going to pass out. She can hear the gurgling noises her stomach makes as it searches for something to digest, and she remembers she has not had anything to eat since breakfast. A snack cart is parked in front of the building, and though she wants only to reach her car so that she can drive away, she stops to finger the puckered skin of an orange, then picks up a hard green apple. "How much?" she asks.

"Fifty cents." The vendor, an attractive young Hispanic woman, holds her hand out for the change.

Reaching into her bag, Lily realizes she has forgotten, among all the other things she has not done, to stop at the bank. "Darn," she says, now truly hungry, her appetite piqued by the promise of the ripe fruit.

When she turns from the cart, an old man calls her back. In her hunger, he reminds her of Perish, the same height, the same lean frame and penetrating gaze, except he has more hair. Matted and unstyled, it hangs down past his shoulders, and his jeans are torn and frayed. "Go ahead, take it." He motions, dipping a hand into his pocket for change. She feels so light that the breeze might just carry her off. "I can't," she says, sensing that he can ill afford this generous offer.

"Go ahead." He purses his lips and juts his chin in her direction.

She does not think she could possibly be as hungry as he looks, and she wonders where this gesture of kindness comes from.

He juts his chin again.

"Thank you," she says, taking him in again to make sure what she's seen. *I owe you. I wish I could pay you back,* she wants to add, taking a big bite of the apple and turning away.

Driving home, Lily recalls how vivid Joseph appeared at the autopsy. The sight of him bending over the man has offered her something unsettling and unexpected, and she wonders why it is that her husband should seem most alive when presiding over a dead body. She sees him dropping his surgical mask to blow her a kiss, and then her thoughts turn oddly again to Perish, the way his eyes fastened on her earlier in the day, and the images of both men combine inside her.

Joseph arrives home that night just as she is tucking Jessie and Misha into bed. "Read us another story, Daddy," Jessie begs, not missing a beat when she glimpses Joseph in the doorway.

"Grrrr, I'll eat you up," Joseph roars, racing into the room with his arms outstretched.

"Achhh," Misha screams.

"No, no, I love you so," Jessie chants. Only she can break the spell, protect her little brother from the wild thing, and perhaps entice her father into fulfilling her wish because she is so charming and smart.

Lily laughs as Joseph hugs the children, planting kisses on the cheeks of both, then winking at her. He takes her hand, and they walk together out of the children's room; then he embraces her in the hallway. As if daring her to observe how neatly death can reside between them, he presses her to his chest, bathing her in the sour odors of his day. "It was nice of you to drop by today, a nice surprise. But why didn't you wait for me? I wondered after you'd left whether I'd seen you at all."

"I was there all right." She grimaces.

"Well, now you've seen what I do firsthand."

"Yes."

"Was it okay? I mean, did it upset you to see the autopsy?"

"Surprisingly"—she pauses—"no."

"Good," he says, and he leans forward to kiss her.

In a dream she's had twice now, she is moving away from land on a large ocean liner. The hull is partitioned into countless sections that lead up and down, in and away. Her room is located somewhere in the maze, and she is running toward it as the ship pitches on the waves, past a dark room at the end of the hall where an old man sits watching a yellow bird in a rounded wire cage, past a bar where the bartender stands idle, past tubs where passengers soak in briny water. She wants to stop running, to explore the ship's interior, but her feet carry her past door after shut door, down endless narrow corridors, and she knows she cannot stop moving.

Not yet.

She wakes up thinking of the children, who will need new pants. She has noticed bare patches that will soon be holes, and cuffs creeping up ankles; it will snow soon, and they will need hats and mittens. So much that has gone undone, or has not been done properly.

A department meeting has been called, and Perish asks her to meet him beforehand for an early dinner. It's an important shift, she thinks, from casual flirting to dinner, and she knows she might have made a mistake in accepting the invitation. She tries to anticipate the night, packing pictures of her husband and children in her handbag as proof of her integrity. At the last minute, though, she can't find the shoes she wants to wear. She could settle for the flat black pumps, she knows, or the Italian loafers, but she has her heart set on the red ankle boots, and she spends more time looking for them than she should.

Angered by having to make a last-minute substitution, she breezes into the kitchen, barely pausing to kiss Joseph and the children good-bye; then, stopping to check on her father one last time, she notices the red tip of a boot protruding from beneath the bed.

"What are my boots doing in here?" she asks accusingly.

Yas smiles, but he doesn't respond. Lily bites her lip to keep from shouting at him, demanding to know why he's taken to hiding her things, and by the way, is it deafness or just the usual preoccupation that keeps him from answering her questions. She refuses to look at him, but she can swear he's watching her change shoes, visualizing the spot under the bed where now she sets her loafers. "I'll get these later," she scolds, blaming him for more than just the missing shoes and how late she's going to be.

"I like your boots," Perish says from the corner table where he sits waiting for her. She smiles self-consciously down at the ribbing of the boots, noting the way they curve into serpentine tips, not thinking of her father at all.

"Tell me about your wife," she says while her foot moves involuntarily. Heel, toe. Heel, toe. Clack, clack, beneath the table in a beat that soothes her.

"She is probably the most brilliant person I've ever known. And she's beautiful."

"My husband," she sighs. "I married him because he's so smart. And attractive. And my children." She reaches into her bag as if on cue and pulls out the photos of her family. She smiles lovingly at the image of her children, their spectacular wholeness. "They're a dream."

She chews her pizza and gulps down beer in the noisy restaurant full of cheerful strangers and talks about her life. She is enunciating each word as if her life depends on speech until the lights overhead appear to be dimming and she feels dizzy. She wants to ask him if he's ever felt like dust, fragmented and free-floating through the air, but the next thing she hears is his voice.

"You look unwell," he is saying, his eyebrows arcing in concern, and she wonders what she's missed.

"This pizza." No longer hungry, she stares down at the mass of cheese and vegetables. "It doesn't taste right."

"Have more beer," he says to her, and she brings the cold glass to her lips.

She is only as close to him as he is to so many others around him, and the air smells heavily of garlic and wool. The sky darkens; perhaps it will snow. It is cold out, but she can feel sweat along her hairline, and the bottoms of her feet are hot. Beneath the table, she taps: heel, toe. Heel, toe, against the smooth hardwood floor, and a chill makes her body shudder.

"So how did you get a name like Perish?" she asks, suddenly suspicious of the old, familiar-looking man sitting across from her, and curious, too. She thinks, *Failing, passing, dying, dead,* and begins to laugh. "I'm sorry, but I can't help but wonder what kind of parents would choose a name with such morbid connotations."

"I'd never thought of it that way." He cocks his head and momentarily says nothing. Then he begins to laugh, too. "It's not my real name, but I guess the name I was given is even more moribund."

"Oh?" She feels warmed by her laughter and the beer.

"My given name is Perry, as in Commodore Matthew C. Perry. As in 1853." He tips back his glass, never taking his eyes off her, letting the last of the beer foam trickle into his mouth.

"Oh." She winces and notes the bumps and creases on the length of his exposed neck. "Ouch."

"You have to remember, I'm a bit older than you." He waves his finger in midair to signal the waitress, then holds up his empty glass. "I was born right after the war. My parents had been interned. They'd lost everything, and anti-Japanese sentiment on the West Coast was still raging. In a situation like that, innocence is never enough. They had to show that they were *super* Americans.

"And they thought Perry Ishida had a nice ring to it."

Lily smiles, but her mind lags behind the conversation. "My mother was interned, too," she muses. "Her family was relocated from California to Heart Mountain, but they moved to upstate New York after the war because her father was offered work there."

The waitress places a full glass of beer in front of Perish, and he holds it up, putting an end to the information Lily has offered about her parents. "To what we share." He raises his glass.

"You're right, you don't look like a Perry," she says after she's sipped at her beer, letting *Per-Ish* find a spot in her head.

"They set me up to be a historian," he moans, and then, changing the subject, "So what made you decide to become one?"

"Funny you'd ask that," she says. Averting his eyes, she recalls again her first semester of college in New York. Afraid to look up at the buildings that were so enormous they blotted out the sky, the storefront windows with size-ten shoes that always reminded her of coffins when she walked past them lit up in the dark. Then returning home to her parents. The snow came down in clusters all that bleak gray afternoon, and she'd watched it from the solitude of her bedroom. She'd fallen asleep watching it and not woken until she heard her mother's voice calling her for dinner. Rising from her bed, she could see that the sky was dark, the room lit only by the whiteness of snow, and she wondered why she felt so disoriented by a scene that should have felt familiar. Before making her way down the hall to answer the questions she knew her father would have for her, she pressed her back to the cold windowpane and asked for a sign, a direction in which to move her life, and a sheet of white paper drifted down from a high shelf above her desk and landed in front of her, and she stared at it, knowing somehow that her task would be to fill it.

It could be that the air circulating through her room caused the paper to fall; it could be that the blank paper meant nothing, or that it meant something other than what she interpreted it as. But she held to it, and at dinner when her father demanded to know what she planned to make of her life, the blank sheet turned to bird's wings fluttering over the dinner table, casting shadows over the string beans while her father awaited an answer. "I'm going to be a historian," she told him, refusing to disguise her enthusiasm. "I'm interested in knowing the origins of things."

He'd just laughed; her father, who did not believe in signs.

It has been almost half her life since she went away to college, or lived through those dreaded dinnertime conversations, but now she relates the story to Perish, who seems somehow capable of embracing her humiliation along with her hopefulness, and sitting across the table from him, she doesn't know whether she'd like to call him closer or send him away.

. . .

Thanksgiving weekend she discovers she's lost her house keys. Unable to think where they might be, she blames her twenty-two-month-old son, can see him wandering off with the keys, fitting them into cracks in the brick floor, spaces between the adobe bricks of their walls. Finally she remembers leaving them on the roof of the car as she slid the baby out of his car seat, hungry and crying. "I left them on top of the car," she cries to Joseph.

"Oh, no. When?"

"Friday!"

"Well, they're gone, then." He shakes his head disapprovingly, and she recalls places they've gone since Friday: lunch, the bookstore for a children's reading, shopping, a day trip north to Santa Fe for her father.

"They're gone," she repeats, remembering the silver feather her husband had bought her on the streets of Manhattan seven years back, during their first year of marriage. It had cost twenty dollars, more than they could afford at the time, and it dangled on a leather rope around her neck. She liked the heat of the metal against her chest, and she had worn it until the night their first child was born, when she took it from her neck and placed it in her jewelry box for safekeeping. She thought to put it back on, but she never did. Instead, because she misplaced her keys over and over, each time crying because of her inability to hold on to anything, Joseph had cut the leather jute and tied the feather to a key ring with a strand of liquid silver. "There now." He recycled a new gift out of the old one. "This you won't lose, right?"

As if to show her faith in him, she kept the key ring with the feather through the birth of their first child and the birth of their second, through the move west, kept the key ring with the feather for over five years, and now it's lost, and with it some part of her history with him defiled.

Joseph disappears into the garage and reappears, dangling the keys high above his head like a trophy. "You're lucky," he says, and he takes her outside and shows her where the feather attached itself to the luggage rack of the car and stayed fastened there through the busy weekend.

"I'm lucky." She hugs him in the garage, and when he has gone back inside, she climbs up on the roof of the car and inspects the unlikely place where the feather got stuck. At sixty-five miles an hour, the keys could have flown off, or someone could have stolen the car, or she might not have remembered she left them there at all. She cannot be sure what it means to have lost the keys and discovered them again, but she feels certain of meaning hidden there.

"A sign," she tells Joseph, "of good things to come."

The first two weeks of December are crucial to finishing off the academic term well. After teaching, when she is not rushing off to pick up her children and tend to her father, she spends the days in her office reading. Finals must be given, papers graded and handed back. But lately her work is not getting done. Misha will turn two soon, and in anticipation of his second birthday, Lily has decided to wean him. She remembers being pregnant for the first time and worrying that her body would not produce milk.

Remembers staring down at her breasts and trying to imagine milk flowing from them. The idea seemed preposterous then, and she was certain she would nurse only for the requisite six weeks. Who could have guessed that the feedings would continue for two years? Or that for the next five years, she would be pregnant or nursing a baby?

It seemed like nothing short of a miracle when the baby cried and milk swelled her breasts. She had only to think about her baby for the milk to come down. She's learned a few things about babies in the last five years, knows for one that for optimum milk production, the mother must work in concert with the baby: when the harmony is broken, there is either not enough milk or too much. Now her breasts are full with milk that she will not let Misha suckle, and she wishes it would somehow go away. She is tired of staring down at pages that must get read before morning and feeling as if her vision is blurred by milk. She should be in her office reading, not sitting outside on a cold bench with an unread prospectus beside her, arms wrapped tightly across her chest, when Perish appears out of nowhere. She hears him say, "You need a cup of tea," and for lack of an appropriate refusal, she smiles up at him and follows him to the tea shop.

This time he does not ask about her life. He talks instead about how he grew up shooting things. Tin cans, car tires, quail, rabbit, deer. She has never shot anything besides a target at an arcade she went to with a boyfriend as a teenager. She has never held a gun, except a fake one, has always felt squeamish about guns; but today she is interested, wants mostly to know from Perish what it feels like to kill something, though she can't locate this desire within herself.

"There was a time when I could say I'd killed everything I ate, but I can't say that anymore," he says.

"Yes." She nods. Having spent two pregnancies choosing free-range chicken and organic cuts of beef, she can see the value of knowing what you eat, only that's not what he's talking about. "I mean," she says, "I wonder what it's like to kill a living thing. To look an animal in the eye and then shoot it."

"It's something I grew up doing." He shrugs. "I don't do it anymore."

She sips her tea. Perhaps he has come to claim the space being vacated by Misha, she thinks. Even though her aim is to separate from her baby, she feels preoccupied by him; she can still feel him like a weight in her chest and a thickness in her limbs that makes her movements slow and ponderous.

It's while Perish is talking of shooting things that she remembers seeing him for the first time. "The cranes," she gasps, realizing that she met him when she visited Albuquerque as part of her job interview. "My outing to the Bosque with the department. You were there, weren't you."

He smiles. "I remember everything about that day."

"You're the man with the onocular." She throws her head back and laughs. "How come you didn't say anything to me?"

"I'm shy."

"You are?" She gazes through the dirty window, trying to understand what he could possibly mean, and trying, too, to remember. "I don't recall your saying much to anyone. I don't think I knew you were part of the department. But I thought you were very distinguished. A visiting scholar, perhaps. Foreign, I thought."

Now a context has magically been created, a past shared unwittingly, and Lily's imagination summons an image of what they saw together that day. "It was the goriest thing I'd ever seen," she says.

"Yes."

"I'm talking about the coyote."

"I know."

"It snuck up out of nowhere and devoured that crane. You saw it, too, remember?"

"You hardly ever get to see such a thing."

"It's not anything I'm likely to forget."

"No." He laughs again. "I remember you. The way your hands covered your face, how you didn't want to look until it was too late to see anything, and then you didn't want to stop looking."

Weaning Misha is, she decides, like killing something. She thinks of the way he slept in her bed for the first months of his life, turning toward her in the middle of the night for milk and warmth. How later he could sleep the night through without being fed, but still needed touch to know he was safe. She can feel the warmth of his baby fingers as he slipped inside her shirt like a lover, patting her chest with a self-satisfied grin. This isn't the way it was when he was an infant; this behavior, she knows, is no longer appropriate. Soon it will be embarrassing, and though he clings to this comfort he's always received, he needs to stop. In weeks, maybe even days, he will be fine. In a year, he might not remember having suckled from her breasts at all. But she will remember. She feels old. Her second and last child is no longer a baby, but sitting across from her, Perish looks at least a dozen years older, his hair thinning, the color fading from what was once black, like hers.

I am in love with you," Perish confesses not long after the tea. It is the middle of a late fall afternoon, and they are sitting at a bar she has never been to. She has no idea where she is, though she stared out the window of his truck, tracing the familiar path of streets, routes that she has taken with her husband and children to get elsewhere. Along the road she knew so well, he turned off while she was looking down. As they navigated the parking lot, which appeared vast with its rough gray asphalt and white lines appearing from beneath the ice, she was struck by how different everything looked in the snow. Now, in the bar with dark wood paneling, glass casts reflections off the tables, and walls appear steeply angled in the cluster of small rooms. He has picked a long booth, big enough to seat eight, but the table is so narrow that she could easily reach across and touch him.

"I am in love with you," he says across the table again, after they have talked about work and other things she won't remember. "But there's something you should know about me."

She thinks *death;* she thinks *disease.* She sees her parents' car, metallic under the moon, barreling down the thruway, just seconds before the crash.

"Look," he says.

She turns her face away, letting her long hair drape the rounded corner of the table. She can feel time suspended in the rows of wineglasses that hang upside-down from the low ceiling, see the fragile stems stretching up over curved bowls, how their lips throw reflections at one another, toss light into prisms of color and illusion. She feels herself falling again, and for reasons she cannot imagine, her mother appears before her. It is a face she has not seen in years, but she remembers how, many summers back, they hiked together into the Sierra wilderness, a day trip during a long summer vacation spent at Yosemite. They were not far from Tuolomne Meadows, their destination, when her mother suddenly collapsed. It might have been dehydration, coupled with the heat of the summer afternoon; she had lain unconscious in the dirt for no more than a minute, but what she spoke of afterward was an experience like what Lily imagined of death. She had entered a tunnel that shone with light at one end, and decided not to press forward, but to turn back into darkness, fighting her way through sticky cobwebs to where she heard Lily's voice calling her. Placing her mother's head in her lap, Lily panicked at the sight of her closed eyes as she twisted her neck against forces Lily could not see—the heaviness of her mother's head in her lap, the fragrance of her hair as Lily brushed it back and called to her. Ahead, through thick, knotted pines, lay the meadow, and Lily could see patches of grass and orange poppies drifting in the open air. Gazing beyond the sharp-tipped pine needles, she longed to be there, in the vast space and sunlight, and she wondered why their hike had come to an end just short of their destination. She recalls the blackness of her mother's hair and the smoothness of her skin and thinks how young her mother had been at the time—young and beautiful and vivid at an age not distant from Lily's now.

Turning back to face Perish, she does not flinch when his palm glides across the table and his fingers brush the hollow beneath her cheekbone.

She reaches a hand up to her own cheek to remove his hand. "I don't know if I—" she says back, but his fingers slide from her grasp down across her lips.

"Look," he says again.

"What?" she says.

His hand moves to the back of her neck. His fingers are warm and rough. They press against the hollow where skull meets spine until her head drops down beneath the table. The gesture is a forceful one, and with her head pinned momentarily where her shoulders should be, she feels stunned. Beneath the table, it is too dark to see anything. It is dark until he lets go. Her vision adjusts while he reaches both hands under the table to pull up his left pant leg. "I'm not perfect like you," he says, exposing for her view a mass of silver metal and screws.

"I didn't know," she says, coming up for air, her breath stuck somewhere in her throat. "I honestly didn't know. How could I not have known?"

He shrugs.

"How did it happen?"

"Long story," he says. "Do you think you could love me?"

Lily does not hear *love*. Sees instead the gap where the leg should be but is not. Just beneath the pant leg, hidden from view but exposed now to her.

"How could I not know?" she says again.

"I haven't ever shown anyone."

Why? she wants to ask. But she thinks she knows. Something more happened on the afternoon her mother fainted, and she dredges her memory for information. There along the trail, not far from the open meadow, surrounded by the shrill cry of cicadas, tall trees creating patches of shade along the path. The scent of pine and fir hangs in the hot summer air with pollen and dust from the trail. Her mother's neck twists. Dirt collects in her hair. When the spasms stop, Lily smooths back the hair, wiping away a line of spittle that runs from the corner of the mouth to the ear. *It will be all right now,* she thinks as the lids slowly part. *The scary part is over.* But there is something she's forgotten. A group of hikers approaches. They are boys, not much older than Lily. She hears their footfalls and the murmur of voices that breaks constantly into laughter. Then she smells it, the unmistakable odor. In the same instant, her mother's gaze focuses, and two of the hikers hover over Lily, who crouches above her mother.

"Need some help?" The voice radiates concern and goodwill, but Lily never takes her eyes off her mother's face.

"No. Thank you."

"What happened?"

"She's okay," Lily cuts off further questioning. "Really."

She guesses that her mother is not okay. She is doing her best not to respond to the panic that tells her to get help. She is holding her breath to the smell that makes her want to gag and warning herself not to cry. She does not take her eyes from her mother's, but she speaks to the boys. "The heat," she hears herself say. "She seems all right now."

A hand lowers a canteen. Lily pours water into her mother's mouth and uses a few drops to moisten her hair. "Thank you," she says, raising the canteen back up to its owner.

The boys are gone. Her mother rises unsteadily and disappears into the brush. When she returns, she does not speak of the incident except for a stern remonstrance. "Daddy doesn't need to know about this."

"But are you okay?" Lily is crying.

"Of course I'm okay." Her mother's voice is matter-of-fact, forbidding further questions.

There is nothing between the two of them to cover the brown stain, but perhaps it has been absorbed into the pattern of the fabric. Lily doesn't look. Has no more memory of that afternoon, or of a context for the story her mother later told of fighting her way back through the cobwebs, though Lily is sure of the story.

Now Perish stares at her from across the table. His eyes are hungry, desperate. She does not know exactly what he sees, but looking into his eyes is like seeing a story she's forgotten until now.

"Do you think you could love me?"

His voice is barely audible, and she hears him pleading with her. There is only one right answer to Perish's question. "No," she says. "I'm married, and so are you."

"I'm in love with you," he insists.

She does not love him. She does not feel anything for him, except perhaps fear, which is both terrifying and terribly exciting. Sliding her hands from the surface of the table, she sees the damp circles left behind by her fingertips.

His hand returns to the hollow beneath her cheek. "I've wanted to touch that spot for a long time now."

She cannot tell if it's excitement she feels or despair, but she has heard his confession and other things, too. Night is coming on quickly as they walk back to his truck. It is twilight, the hour when the sky makes impossible promises, irresistible pacts that will be occluded by darkness and perhaps never renewed but are held nonetheless by a mysterious beauty that envelops everything offered by light. She finds it hard to balance as she concentrates on moving through the snow, one foot in front of the other. She wants to stare down at his legs, to wonder at the way he is able to navigate the ice. She wants to offer her shoulder in case his footing is not steady, but he keeps pace with her. Though he does not reach for her, she can feel that they are already somehow entwined.

He drives east up the bony white face of the Sandias, up past the sun, which has sunk below the Jemez Mountains to the west. A red glow turns deep blue over the horizon, where stars lay hidden inside the darkening sky; they drive past rows of snow-covered houses, with their porch lights burning to where the road ends. He stops the truck, and she reaches across to where he sits, and he takes her in his arms. She is laughing, feeling her thirty-five years as a bone in her hip pops, surprised to assume an unfamiliar angle. She stretches across him, her toes pushing at the narrow tips of her boots against the floorboard. She can feel the heat of his breath, the damp warmth of his mouth searching for hers, but she turns her head away.

"Marry me," he says, taking her chin in his palm so that she is facing him. "I've been waiting my whole life for you, for this moment."

She feels delirious. "You're already married," she says to remind herself.

"So are you." He smiles. "But I've loved you my whole life."

She smiles, too, glancing down at her watch and tilting it to the fading light.

She is late to pick up her children from day care. In the car on the ride home, Misha sings from his baby seat in back, "I miss you this much, Mommy!"

In the rearview mirror, Lily can see the broad smile that reaches across his face, arms extended as far as they will stretch. "I missed you, too, sweetie."

"Mommy?"

Lily looks again in the mirror, this time to the other end of the car to see Jessie, her face somber as she stares off at the dark mountains that resonate through the space between them like an echo. Sometimes Jessie is serious in a way that frightens her.

"I love you," her daughter says.

"And I love you." Lily smiles.

"When you are gone"—Jessie pauses—"I will hold you in my heart forever."

"That's a wonderful thing to say," Lily offers cautiously, "but I'm not planning on going anywhere."

"Yes, you are." Jessie frowns, her pale, round face catching light from the approaching cars like a moon.

Gazing ahead at the stars in the evening sky, Lily wonders what it is that Jessie can possibly see.

"You're getting old," her daughter sighs, "and pretty soon I think you will die."

L ily's father is in the bedroom. He is in the kitchen. He is wandering, and he is waiting for her. "What did you do today?" she asks when the children have settled in and she has taken her place at the stove.

"I worked outside, mostly." He shifts from his position beside the stove, one foot to the other, in a way that makes her think he is guilty of something.

"Oh?" She squints out the window into the black night. "You didn't cut down any more trees, did you?"

She is half joking, but he is utterly serious. "Maybe just one more," he confesses.

"No!" She drops her wooden spoon on the counter and runs out back, leaving the door ajar, flailing through the darkness as if through memory. "Which one?" she yells. "Why?"

At the far end of the property, a shimmering aspen rests on its side, reduced to a stack of branches; a handful of round silver leaves quiver as if gasping for air. Lily presides over the hole where the tree stood, remembering the summer when, only months before, she arrived with Joseph and the children in the high desert happy and safe. The trees provided shade for the children. She had counted fourteen the day they made an offer on the house, and now there are only twelve. Standing over the mangled roots in the snow, she begins to shiver and realizes she cannot stay outside much longer. The frigid air cuts through her skin, and her heart sinks. "Why?" she runs back into the house yelling. "Why?"

"Blight," he says.

"That tree was not blighted."

"It was." He smiles. "But it's okay."

It's not okay, she wants to say, but she realizes her words would not make a difference. Joseph will be home soon, and dinner is not yet under way. She will let him take up the matter with her father. Joseph's profession makes him familiar with deception. He sees daily how the body undoes itself. He will not be easily fooled.

Standing at the stove once more, she does not think of Perish. She takes comfort in the realization that she married Joseph because she can rely on him to uphold her end of a story and to love her fiercely. She will get through this with him, get through this because of him.

Lying awake, Lily sees her mother, immaculately dressed, examining her image in the mirror above the sink. Midori has just come in from dinner and is, Lily knows now, impossibly full. Smoothing the front of her dress, she extends her thumb and forefinger to describe a circle across her belly. "Look," she calls to where Lily sits playing in the tub. "Doesn't it look like I'm going to have a baby?"

Lily, her eyes huge, shifts her attention from her bath play to her mother's protruding abdomen. Then she stares under the water at her own belly. "You're not going to have a baby."

"I don't know." Her mother frowns. "It sure looks like I am, doesn't it?"

Between Lily's hands are bubbles she's made out of the soapy water. Their oily, translucent surfaces hint at color, expanding and contracting as she presses her hands together then pulls them apart. She's never imagined a sibling. There has never been room for anyone else. She allows herself to imagine a sister.

In the days to come, a baby grows in her imagination until her mother appears one night in her room, her face twisted, her eyebrows knotted and thick. "What are you doing?" she demands of Lily.

"Playing." Lily, naive, turns away.

"Who were you talking to?"

"No one." Lily shrugs, guilty for sure, though of what she doesn't know.

"I thought I heard you talking to someone."

"I'm playing with the baby," she says, wishing her mother away.

"What baby?"

Seeing that her mother is genuinely confused and agitated, she rushes to wrap her arms around her mother's waist. "That baby!" She plants a kiss just above her mother's navel, then stares up at the bemused expression shading her mother's eyes.

"What are you talking about? There's no baby in there."

Chagrined, Lily knows instantly that her mother's admonition is justified. The baby is gone; her mother's belly lies flat against the fabric of her skirt. She will not mention the baby again. She's foolish and ashamed of her imaginings. Intimacy, she knows, even at the age of four, exists in the sudden, magical collapsing of space. The stuff between is recognized for what it is: an illusion scared off by heat. This is the knowledge of the body that will bind Lily to her mother forever.

In a dream that night she arrives at the shore, where, high on a platform, a white bird, so small it fits neatly into the palm, is being tethered. A length of cord binds its wings to its body, so tightly that the bird's chest pulses as it struggles to breathe. The day is beautiful, the sky overhead breathtakingly clear, the sun lighting this act of violence taking place on the shore. The small bird is flung like fish bait over the rippling water, and Lily digs her toes into the sand, which is warm and pleasant.

Photos of her children have been lying exposed on countertops and stuffed into drawers where they will eventually be damaged. She has never needed pictures to remind her of her life; it has always been so close. Now she gathers up the photos and brings them to her office, where she can examine them. She is amazed at how quickly they bring her back to Jessie's and Misha's births, picnics and holidays, the move from New York to New Mexico. She lines the photos across her desk and stares at them, feeling that her life depends on proper sequencing, but she is barely able to remember what came first. Something is missing, she thinks, but it takes her a minute to figure out what.

There are photos of Joseph holding up the children, his mouth gaping or contorted as he attempts to make them giggle; photos of Jessie and Misha at almost every stage of their short lives; but in all the stacks, there is not a single image of her.

"Let's use my camera and take some photos," she tells Jessie. She picks up her Polaroid and shows Jessie how to position shots through the viewfinder; then she stands, arms outstretched, back against an adobe wall. "Can you see Mommy in the frame?"

"Yes."

"Okay. Go ahead and shoot."

Her body appears in fragments: her chin, the top of her head, a forearm with hand and fingers, a breast, a foot. Lily gives them to Jessie with a bottle of Elmer's glue, construction paper, and scissors, and Jessie spends the afternoon making refrigerator art.

It's December when seagulls begin appearing at the house. Joseph is the first to notice them, remarking that this type of occurrence is highly unusual. Lily watches through the window as the gulls perch on the wooden posts that hold in the vegetable garden, swoop down from trees to grab in their clumsy beaks rotting carrots and stale bits of bread left out by the children.

From where do they come, these predators so often associated with the sea, and how is it that they have landed in the desert?

A date is set. Perish owns a house in the mountains where his family vacations in the summers. Lily will cancel classes, make excuses to her husband, and drive to his house. She wants to tell someone about her plan; perhaps she wants to be dissuaded. But even more than that, if she can't tell anyone about him, how can she know for sure that he is real, not pulled from her imagination, a fantasy?

Joseph's entrance into Lily's life put an end to her grieving, made her mother's death seem final. But now she can see that it was only a temporary end. That what is lost cannot be regained is Joseph's truth, not Lily's, and these days Perish's missing leg is the thing that makes him real. A paradox, she thinks, that the missing thing should be what is most present between them. Like the treasured possessions her mother lost as a child when the war came, like Lily's own personal history lying hidden and muted until now.

Lily wants Perish to be real, but she knows that reality does not accommodate deviance. There are logistical problems that delay her visit. The threat of snow, the possibility of children, and, when she arrives at his house, a suspicious dog. She hears barking before the door swings open and she sees Perish's face. "Don't mind the dog," he says. "He barks at everyone; it's his job.

"Come in." He bends awkwardly over the dog, hooking a finger through its collar and pulling it back. Still the dog growls, its tail down, feet squared on the white carpet in a defensive posture.

She looks past the dog to a large, open room that spreads out beyond the entryway. It's immaculate: white, bright, and not what one would expect for a country house.

"Your wife is very orderly," she says, and she reaches a thumb and forefinger to the corners of her mouth to stop the trembling there.

"My wife is a slob." He smirks. "But she's lucky, because I'm very orderly."

"Oh." Lily wraps her arms around herself, not sure what to do with the stray parts of her body. In the fireplace, logs hum and crackle, making her suddenly aware of how cold she feels. Though the sky overhead is still and blue, fresh snow casts a crisp brilliance to the landscape as if to sharpen the chill. She is about to go to the fire, wants to disappear into the shooting orange flames calling to her, but Perish places a hand on her shoulder, pulling her back.

"I thought you might like to wear these," he says, producing a pair of house slippers. She looks past them to the floor where, behind the slippers, lie three pairs of shoes; the right sides mashed down and worn with wide-gaping openings that recall a foot; the left shiny and narrow, as if never occupied. They look strange, lining the foyer in imperfect pairs. She knows she should take off her shoes and place them alongside his, but she prefers to keep hers on, snow-trodden though they may be.

None of this is what she expected, and as if sensing her discomfort, Perish shuts the door behind her and walks her to the fireplace. He clears throw pillows off a sofa, but she prefers to stand facing the fire, hoping the image of the shoes and the house behind her will fade away.

"No trouble finding it?"

She wants to say how finding this place has been like leaving Albuquerque for upstate New York. How, in thirty minutes, she's traveled back eighteen years. How this day has suddenly turned into a life she thought she'd forgotten. "No."

"I was worried you might be lost."

"No." She smiles, determined to change her mood. "I hate to say it about myself, but I'm awfully good at following directions."

"I thought you'd never get here. I imagined you in a car wreck, bleeding and unconscious somewhere on the side of the road."

Strange lines gather like clouds over his eyes. She can't help but think of the wreck that killed her mother, but maybe she hasn't heard correctly. "What are you talking about?"

"I can't help it." He holds out his arms, but she turns away and stares into the fire. The fact, she wants to tell him, is that she's been sick. Heaving over a toilet in a coffeehouse where she went to think after dropping her children at day care before embarking for his house. There she remembered how, just days ago, he had driven to the end of the road to kiss her. She had listened to the sound of his breathing in the quiet car, and thought how nice it felt to be enjoying such a moment with him, how good it felt right then to be with him. Maybe that had been enough, an irrevocable moment by which they might belong to each other, perhaps forever. A seemingly innocent impulse to drive away from their lives with the windows down, talking and laughing as their teeth chattered from the cold and their own giddiness, speeding past houses lit up in the snow, then stopping to kiss. But this meeting was serious, premeditated. She had known before she arrived what the day held, an act that had not yet taken place and would be sanctioned not only by memory but by an intimacy that would bind her to him, take her away from her husband and children, a state from which she could not return unaltered, and the thought had made her physically ill. Staring into the mirror over the sink in the coffeehouse bathroom, she had asked herself what she wanted. It wasn't really Perish, was it? She needed an answer, but her eyes shone back, glazed and enamored, her cheeks flushed as if the act of retching had somehow made her face more vibrant. She did not see the tired mother of two small children staring back at her. She'd lost the extra weight she'd carried through two pregnancies and nursing, though she was no longer the woman she'd been before the birth of her children. She'd aged, but time had not spoiled her beauty. There was a knowing look to her face that she hadn't seen the last time she looked, and she had to admit that what she saw appealed to her. Blinking into the mirror, she considered as if for the last time turning around, knowing even then that she wouldn't.

"You're beautiful," he says, wrapping his arms around her from behind and pressing his face into her hair.

"Thank you," she says, closing her eyes.

"I'm obsessed with you," he says.

"Perish." She whispers this and follows him away from the fire, through a house that belongs to his wife and children, to a bed he has made for her, the place she will occupy with him.

"Your dog," she says as she watches Perish undress, her breath quickening at the sight of his leg as he unwraps it from the prosthesis and carefully leans the metal frame against the wall. She wonders if it is rude to watch, and wonders, too, at what she is seeing. Part of him so clearly missing. A gap between his kneecap and the ground, filled with nothing but air. She wonders how he can balance, but magically, he does. Without the prosthesis, he is not graceful, but it is as if the loss of the leg has beautified the rest of him.

"Does he go everywhere with you?" Ashamed, somehow, to stare, she asks about the dog.

"He likes it here," he says, standing against the wall in his underwear, perfectly rooted on one leg.

The dog stands at the foot of the bed wagging his tail, as if excited by what he sees. Perish undresses her, casting her clothes on top of his own in a heap on the floor, and the dog sniffs the pile.

There is an instant after he undresses her, a hiatus in which he is not touching her, not yet inside her, when she wonders again what she wants. She has more love than she can return, a husband, two children, three dogs, a cat. What can possibly be gained by continuing? The affair has not yet begun, not officially at least, but that it will end seems already a given. Someone will make a mistake, someone will find out, quite possibly everyone will be hurt. She imagines she can still free herself, a last-minute change of heart, but she is wrong. He is strong and amazingly steady on one leg. Steadier than she, whose right foot kicks involuntarily at the space between his kneecap and the ground. Rather than lying with her on the bed he has made for them, he enters her standing up, his back pressed against the wall. She can feel her hips spreading apart, her womb opening to take him in, and a warmth emanates out of her center as her jaw trembles, then soundlessly releases.

How was your day?" she whispers to Joseph when he arrives home late in the evening. The children and her father are down for the night, and she does not want to disturb the unusual quiet of the house, though she is scared, too, that her voice will give her away.

"Not bad," he responds in his usual buoyant tenor, throwing open the refrigerator door, in search of leftovers. "What did you have for dinner?"

"Spaghetti." She points to the top shelf of the fridge, noting the pasty red sauce and imprint of pasta curling like worms against the clear Tupperware. "You haven't eaten yet?"

"No." Joseph pulls down the spaghetti, then plants himself in the middle of the kitchen floor to eat; he reminds her of a robin sticking its beak into the damp earth.

"Want me to heat it for you?"

"Too hungry."

Lily, her arms folded across her chest, watches as he slurps up long strands of pasta. "Any interesting bodies?"

"Not too many. Did the children go down without a fuss?"

"Not much of one."

Lily pulls a paper towel off the hanging roll, wets the end, and wipes at drops of red sauce splattered across Joseph's white shirt. Too late to prevent stains, but she shakes out the paper towel and tucks it into the front of his shirt anyway. While she works, she tries to concentrate only on Joseph. There should, she thinks, be something just between the two of them. Some special moment made of conversation, something they might have missed, and her impulse is to talk. She thinks that if he would say something to make her laugh, things might be okay. She can feel pressure rising in her throat, yet she can think of nothing interesting to say. "No new stories?"

"Not today."

Perhaps he reads disappointment in the silence between them, because just after she walks away, he calls to her gently, "I love you."

She turns back. "I love you, too."

Biting at her lower lip, she doesn't know whether she's angry or relieved. She's tired, yet suddenly she wants to fight against what her husband brings into the house, knowledge that feels too clinical to be real. She has always lived inside her body. Spent the last years bearing children and feeding them milk produced by her body, and before that—before that, she can barely remember. She was young then, living in a body that gave her pleasure, and that pleasure is no longer linked to her husband. She sees her body reduced to a mass of tissue and organs and knows that in some irreparable way, her marriage is fading, her life as it was is ruined. Still, it seems odd to her that it's not the act of making love to Perish that might destroy her but the secret of it.

Standing close to Joseph, she can smell Perish on her body, feel how his arms encircled her only hours before. His presence is so strong with her that she wonders whether Joseph feels it. She cannot remember the words that passed between them, only the sound of his breathing close to her ear, accelerating as his body moved inside hers.

It makes no sense to her at all, and she wonders if it is her imagination, or if particles of dead bodies still linger on Joseph's clothing and even on his skin, the way she imagines traces of Perish's wife inhabit his body, and so hers. Lily has walked barefoot across the woman's floors and touched her things. She had an awful feeling when they made love earlier in the day; she could see his wife's face and felt briefly that it was she to whom Lily made love and was, at the same time, killing.

"Go wash off," she tells Joseph. But she knows that death is nothing that can be washed away.

The Christmas party is mandatory for the wife of a pathologist. It does not matter that the night is bitter cold, wind chasing gusts of snow into the air with a fury that makes it difficult to breathe. It does not matter that she wishes she were with Perish. There is silence as Joseph drives, and she curses the sitter for making them late. It is a way not to have to think of Misha and how he clung to her, begging her not to leave. "I think he thought we weren't coming back," she mutters to Joseph's profile, scared in this weather that Misha's screams might have been prophetic.

"What?" He glances sideways from the road as if surprised to discover someone sitting next to him.

"Nothing."

By the time they arrive, everyone has eaten, leaving the green and red buffet tables strewn with empty platters. With Joseph at her side, Lily picks at the leftovers, hungry and mildly curious as to what she might have missed.

"What do you think this is?" she asks, sniffing at something rolled up on a toothpick.

"Let me see." Joseph lifts her elbow to steer the meat into his mouth. He smiles. "Must be something from the freezer downstairs."

Lily is horrified. She imagines the floor beneath them where, in the crypt, fifty bodies are beginning to thaw, limbs once frozen becoming agile again, suppleness returning to the flesh. How can Joseph stand to be around so much death? Doesn't it haunt him? What makes someone want to work with dead bodies? She watches his profile carefully as he ushers her through waves of smiling strangers. Can't she be, for one night, the loving wife of the good doctor? It shouldn't be so hard on this occasion, when Joseph is clearly king of the world. Everyone seems happy to see him, and pleased that he looks so handsome and well entouraged. But Lily wonders if people understand how dark he really is. Smart doctors are able to detach their feelings about life from their feelings about death. But the best see life and death as reciprocal; everything is connected, and the connections, they know, are absurd.

"See those candles?" Joseph whispers in her ear. "They're left over from a memorial service. Remember the one for the babies? I think you read about it in the paper."

"Joseph." She wraps an arm tightly through his. "That's creepy."

He laughs. "Yes. It's all creepy, isn't it?"

The atmosphere is festive. Brightly emblazoned colors, faces flushed in the soft yellow light, mouths open and laughing. To-night the pathologists are not wearing masks, but even smiling, their faces all seem gaunt and green from breathing in too many chemicals, their eyes glazed from viewing too much death. They have, in their favor, a sense of humor. But when has it ever been pleasant to be surrounded by so much death?

Halloween, the Day of the Dead, and the Obon, the Buddhist festival of the dead. Perhaps life has always been a perpetual car-nival of death.

"I'm hungry," she tells Joseph, leading him back to the empty tables.

"What would you like?" he asks, checking his watch. "It's not too late to go out for dinner."

"No," she says. "I want something sweet."

"Ah," he says. Gripping her hand, he leads her through the double doors, away from the party, to his office at the end of the hall. It takes a minute for the flickering lights to brighten, but when they do, everything appears bleached white. The first thing she sees is a photo of herself on top of his desk.

"Where did you get that?" she asks.

"I believe it was taken at our wedding," he says, holding the photo in both hands and brushing dust from the wooden frame.

"So it was." She looks over his shoulder at the way the white silk catches the afternoon sunlight. Her smile was radiant, genuinely happy. "We were happy that day, weren't we."

"Yes." Reaching down into the drawer of his desk, he retrieves a box of cookies, elegantly wrapped with a crisp red ribbon. "Have one. From my private stash."

"Thank you," she says. "Where did you get these?"

"That would be"—he tightens his jaw into a closed-mouth smile—"from the mother of a boy who shot himself."

"Oh." She holds the cookie between her clenched teeth.

"She believes that I got the record changed to accidental death."

She releases the cookie from her teeth. "I don't understand."

"Insurance companies won't pay out on a suicide. The boy was messing around with a gun, but she doesn't think he meant to kill himself. It wasn't possible to tell for sure."

"I see." She relaxes into his high-backed chair and scans the room, its corners joined by framed certificates and diplomas, thick medical books and the fragments of a human skull. A wall plaque reads, *We are seekers of truth, not makers of cases.*

"It's nice in here," she says. "You have a nice office."

"It's not bad." Joseph pulls her up from the chair and, encircling her in his arms, begins a playful dance as music from the party seeps in through the walls. "Merry Christmas," he murmurs.

"It's not Christmas." She laughs, thinking how soft his cheek feels against her lips and how good he smells.

"I know." But tonight he is a magician. He can make the light dissolve. With one hand held behind her waist, he can flick a switch and make the entire world shift or even disappear, with the certainty that nothing can remain unchanged.

Two

L ook at me," he commands, and she realizes that her eyes have been shut. Seeing him is like standing at the edge of a deep, fast-flowing river. The gap between kneecap and ground scares her. The lines and pits in his face scare her. His eyes are liquid, too filled with longing for her when he is that close. His face, inches from her face, calling to her.

Theirs is the light of darkness, a slit through thick drapes at the Four Winds Motel, a bent white ray of light that spreads through the room in patches of gray. It is not ideal, but it is familiar, along with the stiff pillows and rough white sheets, the nubby blankets and ugly floral bedspreads cast in a heap at the foot of the bed, the mirror fastened solidly above the dresser, recording their movements. She watches as he embraces her, sees his biceps sliding down her back to where his elbows meet her waist, his forearms connecting with hands encircling her buttocks. She thinks of her son, the way he begs to ride the carousel again and again, each time with perfect posture, never smiling, never unlocking his fingers from the pole to wave back at her or Joseph as they call to him from the crowd. She remembers asking Joseph once what fantasy he thought Misha could possibly be having from atop his painted pony. Her husband had shrugged. *Another historian in the family.*

Lily can see sweat glisten in a soft patina that lights their bodies. She knows that Perish's fingers, as they trace the curve of her neck, her breasts, her back, are committing her body to memory, and she wonders what happens to this knowledge contained by the body, however wrongly. It's like the hair and nails that continue to grow on a corpse. In giving her body to him, he has become part of her: an extra leg, a missing parent. This is the secret knowledge held by the body, this transubstantiation of flesh.

She remains most interested in his missing leg, and she works her way south to kiss first the leg that's there and then the one that isn't. It stops short, as if it's weightless, a cork dangling in midair, and she cups it in her hands, sucking the flesh into her mouth, then wedging his leg between her legs until he lifts her by the waist and centers her on top of him.

"Tell me what it feels like," she implores him.

"It feels good," he tells her. "You feel wonderful."

She drags her fingernails down his chest in small circles as she moves back down to the leg. "No, silly," she says. "I want to know what it feels like here."

"Honestly?" Movement ceases as he folds his arms into a pillow beneath his head. "It doesn't feel like much of anything."

"No feeling at all?" she asks, coaxing the nub of flesh with her fingers.

"No," he says. "Afraid not. When it first happened, it was wildly sensitive. I could put my hand two inches from the bottom, in the space where there was nothing, and the pain would be so excruciating I'd scream. And as you know I'm not a screamer." He grins.

"Right," she teases.

"But it's the opposite now. Like a tree that's been cut to the roots."

"Hmmm." She doesn't know why this appeals to her. Like the leg that isn't there, what is missing and hidden defines the space between them. Flaws of logic as evident as those of flesh. Straddling the hard mound above his kneecap, she moves herself back and forth, smiling with her eyes closed. "What if I were to do this?"

The body is the gate through which transcendence passes, and she is fascinated by how it works. The body contains the spirit, holds it, shapes it, releases it, making this act that they commit together, so far from love, a crime. "No one must know," she tells him, a whisper in the dark. "No one can ever know."

"No, you're right," he says.

"Who could have known?" she wonders aloud.

"Who could have known what?"

"Nothing," she says. She doesn't want to admit to herself how much she has come to crave his touch. She knows that desire is skewing her vision. Why else would she risk everything to be here with him?

"You smell like olives," she tells him. The rich, oily smell of his skin as she presses against him, fusing his scent to hers. "When I get home tonight, I'm going to open a jar of olives and eat them all and think of you."

"You smell like sea foam," he says. "Like the froth that rises from the ocean and catches in the breeze. If you leave me, I'll move to the ocean just so I can always be near you."

They leave the motel together, her body still arching against his.

"Please don't ever leave me," he begs her.

"Okay," she says. "Good-bye."

He is old, she reminds herself. As she drives away, she fears somehow that he is already a memory. He is a premonition of what is inevitable, a fighting against time for what will soon be lost, a coaxing into life of passion that rises up, then ebbs like a waning pulse. She wishes he could live forever; he wishes he had met her twenty years ago. Twenty years ago he was whole, he tells her. Twenty years ago she was a child, she wants to tell him, but she doesn't.

The mirror is a magnet, and her body is pulled taut by its reflection. She likes to stare; it doesn't matter where she is. Doesn't matter if the light overhead is yellow and false, or if the image produced by glass is tinted, dulled, or distorted. She raises an arm, and it pleases her how pale the skin is there, untouched by the desert sun, the way a line of muscle attenuated from armpit to elbow can whisper like a long, slow song. She runs her fingers through her hair and feels her nails rake her scalp and sees the rivulets of flesh that shine beneath the blue-black stream. Someone looking on might guess that she is in love. But attraction is not love, not necessarily. It is not like Misha, who watches himself in the bathroom mirror every morning while she brushes his hair and teeth. She admires his staring, so persistent that it sometimes makes them all late. The way he scrunches his nose, flutters his eyes beneath his curly brown lashes, then peeks from between outstretched fingers and laughs as if recognizing himself for the first time. It is not like Misha, because she has a long-standing relationship with her body. She marvels at her chest, remembering how, when she was a child, her nipples lay flat against her rib cage, sometimes even inverted from the cold; how her breasts, once swelled with milk, have sunk tightly back into her chest. She likes the way age has drained the fullness from her face, likes the hollows that appear under her eyes and cheekbones, her clavicle that juts under her neck like a weapon, hidden just beneath the skin.

She knows the mind creates a story that can horrify and pervert what is real yet inescapable. All that cannot be stopped. But the body, bending and flexing to its own rhythm, demands something different.

There is suddenly an explosion of sex in her house. She feels it when she dresses Misha, stretching the tight neck of his shirt around his head. "Where's Misha?" she asks playfully, and he begins tugging, too, grunting until his round head pops through.

"There he is!" He laughs.

Jessie confesses as they drive to school that going down hills excites her. "Let's do that again," she squeals. "Let's go down hills all day!"

"Why?" Lily asks.

"Because it makes me tingle inside!"

Why not? Lily is sure Yas would walk through the house with his genitals exposed if she forgot to lay out underwear for him. The dogs roll together in the back, licking and biting at one another. Her husband wants sex from her constantly now.

She wakes just before the sun, her heart ticking a steady, quick beat. Her eyes open, and she reaches behind her. She wants to feel Perish and is surprised to find Joseph. She knows that it's Joseph not by touch but because even after a night of sleep, his breath smells sweet and falls evenly in her ear, like Misha's breath when he slept between them only months before.

She tries to think of her husband, about whom she has not thought much in weeks; she wonders if she was ever in love with him. She remembers how Joseph pursued her, appearing on street corners, in cafés, courting her on long walks, over dinner, on the telephone. How romantic he was, and reliable.

"Adults make choices," he argued when she told him she never imagined herself getting married. "If you love me, you should marry me. I want to be with you forever."

And because she felt for the first time in her life undecided—and because she felt good being with him and, in his presence, her life felt right again—she agreed.

She remembers the ceremony, held on the North Shore of Long Island, with her father absent and both of Joseph's parents as witnesses. The officiant, whom neither Joseph nor Lily had met before the ceremony, recited words about gratitude, and Lily sucked in the sweet smell of freesia and tuberoses and the heavier scent of the ocean, which rang in her ears, muffling the exchange of vows. Her breathing was broken and shallow, and she cried so hard she couldn't see Joseph through her tears, which left salt stains on her silk gown. The ceremony was short, and their life together then proceeded in a clear, linear fashion with the children, born three years apart, his career, and her teaching; no downtime to think about the past. She lived with the knowledge that each day was fleeting, yet her life was full and the future seemed secure and infinite in its possibilities, the sadness she'd dwelled on too long finally behind her.

Though Joseph might one day be tempted, she doubts he would ever betray her, and she knows without having to ask that he would not tolerate her betrayal of him. In marrying her, he has vowed to make her life beautiful, to make her happy, and to love only her. He will delight in her smile and protect her from harm to all eternity. With his knowledge of death and his belief in life's immanence, he will hold her up. She has betrayed him, but this knowledge, not yet held by her mind, lags like a shadow behind her body, and she wants intact what has already been destroyed.

Cradled in the arms of her sleeping husband, she takes in the air he breathes out, wraps herself in his warmth, and coaxes her body back into sleep.

"I hate you." Jessie glares.

"You're stupid," Misha spits back.

"Enough!" Lily intercedes from across the room, frowning at her two children, still dressed in their pajamas. Their hair and teeth have not yet been brushed, and they are fighting over who gets to play with what while Lily and Joseph sit at the kitchen table drinking coffee with Loren.

"I wish you weren't my brother," Jessie taunts.

Misha begins to sob. "You're not coming to my birthday party."

"Enough, I said," Lily repeats. She smiles at Loren, too tired to move as she watches Misha swing his arm limply at Jessie. "What I lack as a disciplinarian is made up for by my profound sympathy toward my children's desires."

"It's hard." Loren smiles back. "No doubt about that."

Lily does not flinch when Jessie lands a solid blow across Misha's face. She believes she understands her children. They are still so young that for them there is no difference between desire and need. Looking into Jessie's eyes, she registers her daughter's emotions because she can feel them somewhere inside herself.

"Go to your room," Joseph commands Jessie.

"No!" Jessie wails.

"Please don't yell," Lily whispers.

Joseph mutters something at Lily, and then to Jessie, "Go now!"

Joseph finds it easy to dismiss his eldest's behavior as spoiled, but Lily sees it differently. She imagines that for children, it is never a simple matter of fatigue or not getting one's way. She can remember being five and the way the whole world began to collapse before bedtime. The feeling of overwhelming panic, the need to fight against the unruly hugeness of a world that could not be resolved or held back. She would sit undressed on the floor of her bedroom, picking shreds of lint from between gummy toes while her mother demanded she get up and put on her pajamas. Defiance was a way to slow the world down, to bring it closer, and to assert her inviolable importance to her mother, who occupied the exact center of her universe. Lily knows that she is still the most important person in her children's world, and that her well-being depends on them as much as theirs does on her. She tries daily to uphold her coveted position in their lives, and not to violate their faith. Yet she worries what it might mean to them that her faith in herself is being dismantled. For as long as she can remember, this faith has been as essential as air drawn into her lungs. But there is a trade-off for possessing it; there are always trade-offs. Now Perish has come to occupy that place once held by faith.

I can't see you anymore," she tells him, pulling him into a corner when their paths cross outside the history department office.

"Why not?" he whispers, glancing up and down the hallway, then reaching for her face. "I'm in love with you."

"I can't see you because you're ruining my life." She clasps his hand in her fingers, bringing it slowly back down to his side. "I was happy when I met you, and now I'm miserable."

"You make me happy," he sighs. "Sometimes I imagine we were the same person, and somehow we got split in half. Now we've come back together."

"I sometimes feel that way, too," Lily says. "I look at your face and see some remote part of myself. But this morning I looked in the mirror and saw you, and I felt like vomiting."

He grimaces. "I feel that way every day."

"Ah. But that's where you and I are different."

"You're right," he says. "I'm sorry."

"I'm sorry, too."

"So let's not see each other for a while."

"A while seems too short," she says, but to herself, she admits as she watches him walk away, it might also be too long.

B ack in her office, sheaves of paper line her desk. She touches the words that scroll across the page, lifeless, heavy, and intractable. Words fall from the spines of books: *Rome, ocean, purple, wind, woods.* She has always believed that words are life itself, though they are no longer enough. Idle thoughts of losing herself in a foreign city, the sound of waves, a blotch of color cast against a mass of tree are not enough. Today each word speaks of responsibility and of her inability to carry through.

She scans the pages of the text she's assigned a group of undergraduates, ponders the secret codes contained in pacts and treaties with the fervor of a zealot studying scripture. *Advantage, preference, privilege.* This is the story of how people get what they want. But once the thing is gotten, what to do with it then?

It is while she is reading that the world falls away from her. She can feel herself going down; perhaps it is what a ship feels when water begins seeping in, water where there should be air. There is not enough air, even though she is breathing fast, feeling the pulse of breath that rushes in from her nostrils and fills her head and lungs. She imagines her heart as a closed fist opening while she sinks down and down, not sure whether the extreme heaviness in her limbs might not be lightness as some part of her is lifted from her body, freed. It is not like sleep, this state that is neither waking nor dreaming.

Her head collapses, wrinkling the page of a book, and when she opens her eyes, she is cold and shaking. She tries again to read the words that have no meaning besides the burden they carry of what must be done and what cannot be undone.

In the stall of the ladies' room where she goes to cry, she over-hears a conversation: "Perish Ishida has a fine ass."

"A dignified ass."

The voices are familiar. Students she's seen whose names she can't quite place. Through a crack in the stall, Lily watches them laugh, their mouths forming tight circles as they apply lipstick and fix their hair in the mirror. Pulling her pants down, she emp-ties her bladder even though it's not really full. *Don't let them think you're here for any reason other than that. Don't let them suspect.* She knows she should pull up her pants and leave, but she lingers in the stall.

On the way out, she notices a pretty graduate student leaving

Perish's office. How carefully she shuts the door behind her, how she straightens her black knit skirt with the flat of one palm and brushes her hair back with the other. Facing Lily with a weak smile, she mouths hello. The imagination must be kept in check, Lily reminds herself. But it is already too late for such a caution.

A t the end of a difficult day of too much death, Joseph stares blindly into the television screen, a bowl of baby carrots nesting in his lap. Lily sits beside him, watching his face as he waves the remote, bright images flickering in his eyes.

"What are you thinking about?"

"Nothing," he says. And then, "Have you ever noticed how some carrots are much tastier than others?"

"No, I don't much like carrots. When I chew them, I plug my nose and swallow as quickly as I can."

"Really?" he says. "Good carrots are delicious. There's nothing like them. But the question is: when you get a good one, do you stop or keep going?"

She shrugs. "I don't know what you're talking about. What are you talking about?"

"Carrots." He smiles, then turns up the volume to hear what pleases him. It may well be that the carrots are not really carrots. Perhaps as the images flicker in his eyes and the carrot breaks down on his tongue, what he is observing and tasting is really another life, one that does not include her. Perhaps this is hopeful. But the fact is that it does not matter. What matters is what she believes: he has found a way to shut the world out and a way to shut her out. He is a sensible man, something she has always known, and his good sense is, for the moment, preferable to her misery.

Sitting next to her husband on the couch, she tries out a triumphant smile and, with it, a set of renewed thoughts to show that it is genuine. She does not notice that Joseph has turned off the television, that he is watching her, amused, while he munches the last of the carrots. "Are you coming to bed?" he wants to know.

She sees him staring, then catches her own reflection in the black television screen. Throwing her hair across his chest, she smells her own scent that catches in his hands, feels the line of her jaw as he traces it with his fingertips. She is still young; her husband still desires her. She does not desire him, she considers as he pulls her to him. *But it doesn't matter,* she reminds herself. *I am not the unhappy one.*

M*y unhappiness doesn't matter,* she resolves finally. Tucked beside her sleeping husband, she finds herself thinking of her mother. With a palpable longing, she attempts as she's done countless times before to carry her mother up through the years. Through Jessie's birth, then Misha's, the move to New Mexico. She is tired. She can no longer see her mother's face, no longer has any idea how to imagine her. Locked in her head is a still image of her mother standing in the entryway of the house in Oswego. It's her only lasting image of her mother, but it no longer serves her. Her mind drifts back to the accident: late fall in New

York, a windy night not unlike early spring in New Mexico. Sleep will not come.

Rising from bed, she is full of rage at her father. For the accident that killed her mother, for his failing mind, which is daily slipping past anyone's grasp. None of this is his fault, but she has always blamed him. And she has no idea why she has protected him for so long.

"Dad." She taps on his door. She can be insistent because he's not sleeping, no longer sleeps nights when the rest of the house is dark. "Open the door, Dad."

"Midori?" she hears him call. It's a name she hasn't heard in years, and she touches fingers to her trembling lips.

He opens the door with a gentle half-smile breaking through the white paste that lines his mouth. In his right hand is a toothbrush that he uses to point to the bed, flinging foam behind him, dripping more as he walks. "Mi-do-ri." He stretches the name across his tongue as if to play with it there. "I was just brushing my teeth before bed."

She should stop, she knows. Should return to her room, take her respite from his dementia, but her anger hasn't been quelled. "It's me, Lily," she says. "Turn around and look at me, Dad. We need to talk."

"Okay, okay." He waves his wet toothbrush over his shoulder. "*Chotto matte.*"

She doesn't know why she should feel chilled that he's mistaken her for her mother when the only really strange thing is that he hasn't done so before tonight. Waiting for him to return from the bathroom, she remembers complaining to her mother

about him. "I hate him," she'd yelled after one of her many arguments with him. Why they'd fought no longer mattered; in those days he argued with her about everything. He was as oblivious then as now, and stubborn. "I hate him!"

"Don't say that," her mother had retorted angrily. "You don't hate him."

"I do. I hate him."

"I told you not to say that." Her mother had begun to weep, which shocked Lily and stopped her short of repeating herself. "Don't say that, because you have to live with him. You don't say that about people you have to live with."

You hate him, too, she'd wanted to say. But there was no proof of it, nothing in her mother's behavior that ever gave her away.

Now Yas returns and sits beside Lily on the bed, wrapping his arm affectionately around her shoulders.

"No, Dad. Stop." She pulls away.

Her father again, he is affronted, apologetic. "It's too much for you," he says with a sudden and rare wave of recognition.

"I hate you," she whispers, her anger already dispelled.

She waits for his response. A film she hasn't noticed before has settled over both his eyes, and she can't be sure whether it's sadness or cataracts.

Before returning to her room, she stops to check on her sleeping children. Jessie's bed leans against the wall, a down comforter tangled in the purple silk coverlet at the foot. Two book corners appear from under her pillow, and next to them a penlight that she reads with at night illuminates her face. Already she is learning to stay awake.

There is heaviness in the air outside the window that promises snow. The first thing Lily sees in the morning is the fruit tree outside her window offering its new blossoms to the sunlight. The branches of the tree are white, covered in patches from a dusting of snow during the night. The shiny new leaves poke through, showing iridescent green against the blue sky.

The snow is melting quickly, leaving the soil damp and rich. Soon it will be time to plant. Lily watches at the window as Yas, still himself in the garden, takes Jessie and Misha outside to explain to them how it will be done. "The earth is composed primarily of three layers," he says between grunts as he taps his foot against the steel rim of the shovel. "There's the surface layer, the topsoil—"

"Humus," Jessie interrupts.

"Hey." Yas looks up quizzically from his serious work. "How did you know that?"

"You told me, silly."

"Well, then, what comes next? Since you're so smart."

Jessie shrugs.

"The subsoil."

"Right. Subsoil," Jessie repeats.

"What we're doing here is mixing the topsoil. Where you live, it's primarily silt. See?" Raising the shovel a few inches, Yas lets the sand trickle down. "We mix it with soil amendment, which contains nutrients, so that the plants will grow and be healthy."

Misha has planted his butt in the dirt, amusing himself with a handful of small twigs, but Jessie listens intently and watches as her grandfather lifts the shovel again and again for more compost to blend into the dirt.

"Haven't you forgotten something?" she says at last.

"No." Yas does not look up.

"The bedrock." Jessie smiles, arms around herself to protect her from the air that is still too cold to stay outside for long. "You don't want to dig so deep that you hit the bedrock, right?"

Yas chuckles. "No. You don't want to disturb the bedrock." He is quiet for a few minutes, and then he cannot resist going on. "I've been doing this for many years, you know. I've planted hundreds of gardens, and I think I still know a little more about planting than you—"

"Jessie, Misha," Lily calls from the window, sensing that the conversation might quickly turn ugly. "It's time to come in now."

"I don't want you two getting sick," she tells her children as she pulls off parkas, mittens, and boots. She wants to explain something to them about their grandfather, but, unable to think what, she concentrates instead on rubbing the warmth back into their cold fingers and toes and, when they are warm, places mugs of milk and plates of chocolate cake in front of them.

W hat's wrong?" Loren asks when the children are down for the night and Joseph is not yet home.

"Nothing." Lily smiles. "Why?"

"Because you don't seem yourself," Loren says. "And you don't look well."

"I'm fine." But Lily can muster only a half-smile.

"Why don't I watch the children so that you and Joseph can go somewhere this weekend? You two never get out."

"No." Lily does not mean for her voice to come out as forcefully as it does. She has explained more than once why she cannot go out. She doesn't like to leave Misha with sitters. Until he began going to day care with Jessie, either Joseph or she had always been with him. They never went to a movie or dinner because Misha needed them. He was just that way. *Was*. But he's no longer a baby. No longer dependent on her for milk. Next month he will turn two. She must begin planning a party for him. She hates birthday parties. But the reason she responds this way to Loren is not Misha. It's Joseph. The thought of going away with him horrifies her now. She sleeps with him every night, but she has not really talked to him in ages. Doesn't even know what she'd say.

Later, curled up in bed with the covers tucked under her chin, she forces herself to remember. The bar that she probably couldn't find her way back to without Perish, late fall snow covering the ground. She'd been flattered by his confession of love, stunned by his revelation of a missing leg, but she could have walked out and not looked back. She *should* have—

She needs him, and she hates that she needs him. The way Jessie and Misha need her. She has let her children down, she is letting her husband down. She must not see Perish again. Late into the night, she wonders how long life can continue on this way.

· · ·

J essie has always been fascinated by the moon. When she was younger, she would point up at the sky, sometimes in the middle of the day, and shout "Moon!" She loved best when the moon rose full and yellow over the tall city buildings, and when it was absent, she craned her head to watch for its return.

The children in Jessie's group at school have been learning about the cycles of the moon: full moon, half- and crescent moon, new moon. Their teacher explains: "Once a month the moon disappears, and that's called the new moon. On that night the moon hides completely behind the earth, but even though you can't see it, it's still there."

Each night Lily takes Jessie outside to examine the moon's shape and chart its movement across the sky. The teacher tells Lily this story at the end of the day: As a final project, the teacher passes out construction paper, scissors, crayons, and glitter, and directs each child to make his or her favorite moon. Examining the results, two of the children begin to bicker. Jessie stands at the outskirts, listening. "There's no need to fight," she says at last. Speaking calmly, moving her eyes sympathetically from one friend to the other, she takes each child's moon and lays them on the table beside hers. "See, each of us has made something special.

"Miranda"—she points down—"your moon is special because it has silver glitter, and sparkly moons are lucky.

"Zachary," she says, "yours is special because it's round, and full moons are perfect.

"But mine—my moon is the most special of all because it's black, and a black moon is always there."

The children don't know what to make of Jessie's remarks, but a silence lingers in the room as they begin their next activity. "She's such a special child," the teacher says to Lily when she arrives to pick Jessie up, "a natural leader."

Jessie's aptitude for leadership is nothing Lily doesn't already know about, but it is the moon that makes her weep. The teacher continues chatting and smiling, proudly unaware that she has disappeared from Lily's thoughts. Jessie is her black moon: all that people who love each other should be but sadly are not.

The seasons are like the moon, forever changing faces, but unlike the moon that disappears for one night each month. Spring follows winter follows fall like clouds moving across a sun that never sets. "Say them," she tells Jessie. "Fall. Winter. Summer. Spring.

"Do you suppose the order ever changes?" she asks, testing.

"No."

"How do you know?"

"Because the leaves fall from their branches and become dirt so that they can come back again in the spring. There is no other way."

Because Lily never knows when she might be called upon to bake a cake, she stores these items in her cupboard: unsweetened chocolate, flour, sugar, salt, baking soda. In her refrigerator she keeps eggs, milk, and cooking oil. After she has bathed and put the children down for the night, she climbs up on a stepladder and pulls down the ingredients, lining them across the countertop along with measuring spoons and cups and a large mixing bowl.

She never knew how to bake before her children were born. Never knew how to cook at all until Joseph. Remembers a time when she kept only vodka and ice cubes in her freezer, fresh pasta and a bag of tart green apples in her refrigerator, and a can of corn and red sauce in the cupboard. Could have lived endlessly on vodka, apples, pasta, and canned red sauce—a perfect balanced diet for a hurried and imperfect life. She stands in the night kitchen and thinks about this as she mixes the batter, chanting a rhyme from one of Misha's books:

Milk in the batter! Milk in the batter!
We bake cake, and nothing's the matter!
Stir it, scrape it, make it, bake it . . .

She remembers Joseph coming home on his birthday one year—the first birthday he spent with her—to find her stretching dough between her fingers, tears and yeast streaking her cheeks. "It won't work," she'd cried, not used to feeling inept, especially when success depended only on following simple directions.

"Yes, it will." Joseph had laughed sympathetically, grabbing an apron and using the bottom to wipe her face before getting started. "The trick they don't tell you is that you need lots of flour." He'd dusted the work surface, and some of the flour billowed into the air and settled in her hair and on her bare feet.

"See?" He patted the dough gently into a ball, making manageable what had seemed impossible. He'd helped her plan and execute many meals that first year. Going to the store with her to gather the right ingredients without forgetting anything—not one simple thing. She'd learned first how to buy for one dinner, and then how to stock cupboards for a week, even two. Nothing had required more concentration than that, or standing in the long checkout lines, which she would have resented had it not been for her discovery of *Ladies' Home Journal,* in which a meal cooked was a dollar saved and a year added to one's life. She pauses to consider how proud her mother would be. But would she?

The chocolate cake rises perfectly in its round pan, and Lily stays up past midnight waiting for it to cool before covering it. *The baker bakes cake till the dawn, so we can have cake in the morn.* She paces the kitchen idly, amusing herself while the children are still asleep, frosting the black moon cake in white and writing *Happy Second Birthday, Misha* in pale blue script.

He is still a baby, still her baby, and when she hears the sheets rustling in his room, she rushes in to watch him wake up. She finds him in his favorite position, legs tucked beneath his diapered butt, which rises in the air like a perfect egg. Rolling onto his back, he extends his arms and legs as far as they will reach. She scoops him up and carries him into the kitchen, where his eyes fasten on a ceramic bowl of fruit. "Pear," he says, pointing, before *good morning* or *milk.*

"You can't have one today," Lily whispers into his ear, drinking in the light sweat that covers his body from sleep. "They're not ripe yet."

"Tomorrow?" he asks.

"No. Maybe by Friday."

Five minutes later, while smacking his lips around a mouthful of Cheerios, he wants to know, "Is it Friday yet?"

"No, baby," Lily has to tell him. "There are five more days till Friday, but today is your birthday. Today you are two!"

"Two," he chants, holding up a hand and wiggling his fingers up and down like twinkling stars.

"Today is your birthday, and soon all of your friends will come to play and sing and eat cake." She sighs, contemplating the long day ahead, and, reaching across the table, kisses his wet-milk cheek.

I guess you could say that today was a huge success." Joseph reclines, his legs resting across the coffee table, a bottle of beer tilted to meet his lips.

"Huge." Lily huffs out a breath. She sits beside him, knees against her chest, surveying the room with its half-floating blue balloons, new toys and stray bits of wrapping paper, glitter and chocolate cake crumbs littering the ground. "It's very colorful. Maybe we should just leave it this way."

"Or vacate the premises and start anew."

"That's too much work. We can call in the dogs to sweep up. We've done enough work, don't you think?"

"Yes, we have." Joseph swings back another sip of beer. "I know. Why don't we wake your father up and put him to work."

They eye each other and laugh. Yas, who often insists on helping around the house, is no better at cleaning than Misha. Both
start out well, loading their arms with toys and setting off
together—one small figure tucked like an afternoon shadow
behind the larger one. Down the hall they go, to return happy
with their effort, arms still full, or to disappear so that they can
make a mess of another room. Yas is best these days when he's
asleep, when Lily can hear his heavy breathing and occasional
murmuring so she doesn't have to worry. But lately he has taken
to wandering in a half-waking state through the night, stopping
briefly to visit each room again and again. After relieving himself—often in the corner of his room, where Lily has installed a
small number of hardy houseplants (pans under the clay pots and
newspapers under the pans in case he misses)—he takes himself
to Jessie's bed. Lily knows when he does this because Jessie calls to
her, "Mom, come get Grandpa!" Or, if she's feeling nice, she
returns him to his bed herself.

One morning Lily found him curled around Misha like a
mother bear. "What are you doing here?" she whispered, slightly
annoyed, having searched the house and yard.

"Ah." He squinted up at her, perplexed and then panicked.

"You're in Misha's bed."

"Misha."

"Yes." She pointed next to him at the baby who rolled out of
his arms, his sleep apparently undisturbed. "Come." She guided
Yas back to his bed.

"Come." Joseph now pulls his wife up by the elbows. "Let's
worry about cleaning tomorrow."

. . .

Yas enters the room soundlessly to gaze over the tangled bodies of his daughter and her husband. Lily does not know
how long he has been listening to her moans (muffled between
pillows because the children and her father are supposedly asleep
close by), watching her body move against Joseph's. He stands
naked, one hand encircling his erect penis; the other fingering the
few long hairs left on his chest, which spread out between his nipples in an ugly strip of gray. The moment she sees him, she is
aware that he has been watching her having sex, but it occurs to
her that he isn't mindful of what he is seeing; rather, he is replay-
ing an event buried somewhere in his warped memory. But perhaps that's only what she needs to believe.

"Joseph," she whispers.

"Lily," he whispers back.

"Look!" she cries, thrusting her face back between the pillows.

"Goddammit." Joseph jerks his head up from where it has
been buried in Lily's neck, bruising her pelvis with his knee when
he shifts to grab a book from the nightstand. "What the fuck are
you, some kind of pervert?"

"Joseph," Lily, lifting her head, grabs at her husband's wrist. "I
don't even think he's awake."

"He's awake, all right." Joseph transfers the book from one
arm to the other, the full weight of his chest settling on Lily,
smothering her as the book sails across the room, hitting Yas in
the chest. He sees it coming, but it is not shame that prevents
him from raising his arms to protect himself. Nor is it pain or

anger Lily sees in his face when, after a protracted moment, he sluggishly retreats.

"Go to your own bed now, Dad," Lily calls after him.

Once he has turned away, she struggles out from beneath Joseph's weight. Tying the sash of her white robe around her waist, she follows her father down the hall. No longer the insidious father, he has become her third child, and she treats him as such, using the simplest language possible to placate him, taking the same safety measures for him as she does for Misha. "You need to go to sleep here," she tells him, patting his pillows while he perches on the edge of the bed, naked except for his slippers. "This is your room, and you need to put your nightshirt back on and sleep here.

"Look," she says after shielding her eyes while he dresses. She holds up the brown bear that he sleeps with, a bear that belonged to Jessie until she passed it on to Misha, and was Misha's favorite before he gave it to Yas. "You sleep here with Brown Bear."

Yas holds out his arms like a child, and surprisingly it is not anger Lily feels, or even disgust for the now ravaged man who once fathered her. She pities him, alone in the world without a wife, lost inside himself in a place where he cannot be reached. She nudges his shoulder gently back into the fluffed pillows, removes his slippers, and watches as he collapses stiffly on his back. Before leaving, she tucks Brown Bear firmly in his arms.

"I don't understand you," Joseph fumes when she slips back into bed.

She remains silent because she can think of nothing to say to him, but he seems unwilling to let the moment pass.

"You can't keep doing this," he says at last.

She wants to ask, *Can't keep doing what?* Is it her tending to Yas that angers him? Or her lack of affection for Joseph that draws her away and never quite brings her back? She hopes that he sees it as her father—let Yas be the problem between them. She has told Perish she will not see him again, she has avoided the many familiar stairwells and walkways that mark his path across campus for over a week, and she feels an ache in her chest as if her blood has turned to mud.

As she falls into a heavy, exhausted sleep, her mind is lit suddenly by deep shades of indigo, ocher, and marigold. She is imagining the new stalks that have recently appeared in her backyard, genus she has not noticed, surging up from the earth to produce an intricate fusion of color overnight. In her imagination, the buds splay open in a dramatic show of life, and she wonders whether the flowers recognize their own fleeting beauty. Once the petals have withered and fallen to the ground, will they be missed? In the same intangible way that a person might miss color, is it possible for a part of oneself to become blind and not even know what's been lost? She has only recently begun to fear that her love of Joseph is dead, but she does not think he suspects it, not yet.

As she and Yas and the children pull away from their home, it is still early morning. The sun has not yet risen over a sky that rims the pine-covered mountains cerulean, then deepens quietly to black. The car motor flutters in their ears like a hungry stomach or a womb. Yas, who has been restless all night, has joined them for the ride because Lily, fearing for his safety, no longer wants to leave him alone.

"Say 'Good-bye, house,'" Yas says to Jessie from the front seat, pleased to feel himself off on an adventure. Their destination is merely the day-care center where Jessie and Misha get dropped off each morning, but until now he has not been present.

"Mommy," Jessie says plaintively from the backseat.

"What?" Lily snaps, betting that her daughter needs to return to use the bathroom, irritated at the anticipation of one more morning delay.

Jessie does not answer. There is silence in the backseat until Lily, turning over her shoulder, sees in the half-light that her daughter is weeping.

Pulling the car off the road, Lily places her forehead against the steering wheel and begins weeping herself. *It will get better,* she wants to say but doesn't. *Everything will be all right.*

Then, having composed herself as suddenly as she fell apart, Jessie makes an announcement: "I think I know what happens when a person dies," she confesses glumly. "Boys become dragons, and girls become trees."

"Why don't they become the same thing?" Lily lifts her head and looks back, distracted.

"Because they don't," Jessie says, and Lily does not dare question her daughter, to whom this fact is so plainly obvious.

"When I die," Jessie sighs, "I will become a tree, and then I will know what it's like to be part of the earth and to see things from the sky."

. . .

I *miss you,* Perish writes in a note. *I want to be with you. Please. I am in love with you. I can't live without you.*

The light outside is blinding. Spring in full force in New Mexico is enough to take one's breath away, Lily thinks. The cholla flower in deep shades of purple beside honeysuckle so fragrant she can taste the sweetness in her hair. She has known him only in the winter, and she wonders what it will be like to squint at him against the sun, the air so warm that their naked bodies do not require even a sheet. Lying still beside him, she can feel the heat rising off his chest. "It's wonderful, isn't it?" he says.

"What's wonderful?" she asks.

"The heat. You. You feel so warm."

"You feel wonderful," she murmurs, burying her face in his armpit. "You smell wonderful, too."

In fact, *wonderful* is probably not the right word. He smells a bit like decay, a sour odor that somehow pleases her, coming from him. She sniffs the thick, slippery sweat along his hairline, the space between his eyebrows, the crevice hidden like a canyon behind his ears. She is looking for something as she continues on down his chest to his navel, then turns him over and tastes the moisture that collects at the base of his spine. "That feels good," he says. Turning him over again, she uses her nose to tickle the skin that hangs on the end of his left leg. She prods and teases it, but he does not respond. His eyes are closed.

"Where have you gone?" she asks.

"I'm right here with you," he says. "I'm imagining you, seeing you with my eyes closed."

"What do I look like?"

"You're beautiful," he says, "perfect. You are so beautiful." He pulls her up to his face and opens his eyes, brushing the hair back from her forehead. "You've changed my life, you know."

"Yes," she whispers, wanting him to shut up. "You've changed mine, too."

"You've really fucked things up for me," she says after they've made love again, sweat cooling their bodies as a noisy fan circulates air through the room.

"I'm sorry," he says.

"I thought when I met you that I could just go on living my life with Joseph and my children. But now I'm not happy making love with my husband."

Lily knows that what she says makes no sense. Joseph is to anyone's eye the more beautiful of the two. His creamy skin, curly blond hair, and freckles, his body powerful in its youth. Perish is all darkness, but it is his brittle and decrepit body that gives her pleasure beyond reason. "I only want you; no matter what happens, I will always desire you."

"There's no going back, is there?"

"No. No going back."

. . .

M any things cause soil to decay," Yas tells Jessie and Misha as he ponders aloud the dilemma of how to get the grass to grow. "Erosion, weathering, the breaking down of living matter."

Lily watches through the window, surprised to see her father magically himself again. "You must pay attention to the soil," he says. "Without good soil, everything will die."

"How do you pay attention to soil?" Jessie asks, staring down at the sprigs of grass that shoot tentatively through the dirt.

Yas bends down and rubs dirt between his thumb and forefinger. Raising a palm to his nose, he sniffs at the dirt, then lets it fall between his fingers. It catches Misha on the head.

"Hey," Misha barks, "you got dirt in my hair."

But Yas does not hear him. "In most cases," he directs his answer at Jessie, "fertilizer would do the trick—a good blend of nitrogen, potassium, and phosphorous. But in this case, the problem is the dogs."

"What did they do?" Jessie shrugs, looking around the yard for her errant pets.

"Dog piss," Yas grunts, rubbing his thick palms into his trouser legs. "Your dogs are peeing on the lawn, killing the new growth. And then they're trampling it, see?" He points from the porch door down to the gate at a rough trodden patch of dirt where the grass does not grow.

. . .

I don't want these pens," Misha shouts at the set of colored markers Lily has brought home from her office drawer and produced from her purse to surprise him.

"You don't have to have them." Lily holds out her hands. She is exasperated, wanting to take the pens back, but Misha begins to cry.

"Go to your room," he says, but Lily refuses. "I want you to go to your room," he tries again.

"You will go to your room," Lily tells him, "if you don't stop talking to me like that."

They go to his room together, her two-year-old and she. Lily sits him on her lap, and he cries into her chest. Then he attempts to explain. "No one is happy."

His declaration shocks her, but she strokes his damp curls, trying to soothe him. "Who's not happy, baby?"

"Daddy's not happy."

"Oh, Misha." She kisses his ear. "Daddy is too happy. Daddy is fine."

"No." He kicks at her, a foot thrust into the air that she catches just inches from her nose. "He's not."

"Don't kick," she remonstrates, clamping his foot in her palm. "Daddy is fine. You don't need to worry about Daddy."

He tries again. "Jessie's not happy."

"Jessie is happy." She smiles, concerned. "What makes you think Jessie's not happy?"

"Misha's not happy."

"Oh," she says, unable to deny this obvious truth. "I'm sorry."

"It's your fault."

She wants to cry but bites her lip. His anger is justified, she knows. "I'm sorry."

"It's not fair."

"You're right," Lily tells him. She must preserve the world he lives in. It's her job, and she's failing him. "It's not fair."

"I'm going to run away," he threatens.

She frowns at him, then smiles. "Please don't do that," she begs, reaching her hands under his arms and tickling, causing him to giggle in spite of his anger. "I'd miss you. Besides, I'd come find you. You know I'll always find you, right?"

Misha nods, shaking a stray tear from his eyelash.

"I'm sorry you're not happy," she tells him. "But you will be happy again, I promise, okay? We will all be happy again. And do you know how I know?"

He squints into her eyes, looking for an answer. Not finding one, he shakes his head.

"I know because I am going to be much more careful. I've been very busy, and I've had to spend too much time away from you. But I am going to spend more time with you, just so I can make sure you're happy."

"Yay!" Misha wraps his arms around her neck, nearly choking her, but it is not unpleasant. At two, he still trusts her ability to make things right.

. . .

T hen Perish's scribbled note arrives in her office mailbox: *My wife . . . I think she might know something. Don't panic, because she hasn't said anything about you. But she's watching me very carefully, so I'd better not see you as we'd planned. I'm sorry. I'll call you as soon as I can.*

Lily reads the note again and again, imagining the confrontation, wondering what it might mean. She uses everything Perish has told her to conjure an image of his wife. She might be violent, might scream, or cry. Whatever the case, she is most dangerous because Perish is scared of her. Lily has seen him wince when he speaks of her, as if suffering excruciating pain. She imagines what it might be like for him to be evicted from his life, and the thought unnerves her.

Her telephone rings late in the afternoon, at home. "Evidently she went to campus looking for me. She called my office yesterday, when I was with you, and then she went looking for me."

"That's not good." Lily hears her words echoing in her ears as she paces down the long hall, cupping the receiver to soften her voice when she walks by the guest room currently occupied by her father.

"She knows I've left her."

"But you haven't left her."

"Ah, but I have."

Perish is not making sense. His heavy breathing evokes thoughts of an obscene caller, tempting Lily to believe the man on the other end of the line is not Perish at all.

"She accused me of ruining her life," he sobs pitifully.

Catching the sweet scent of her children as she passes the

open door to their room, she can feel her panic mounting. She has been so careful, so certain of her power to conceal the affair. What she hadn't considered was that her own attentiveness might not be enough to protect her. Perish will ruin everything for both of them if she doesn't start thinking about him—thinking *for* him. "Okay." She begins sorting through the mess. "You've done something to make her suspicious."

"She hates me," he whines.

He's not even listening, and it's clear to her that she's getting nowhere until she suddenly understands what she's overlooked. "You've had affairs before, haven't you," she demands.

"What?" He is clearly surprised.

"Your wife—she's suspicious because you've had affairs before and she found out. I'm right, aren't I."

"Lily, you're scaring me." His voice is barely audible. She imagines this is because he's dropped the receiver to his chin, his mouth agape.

"Perish, I don't care that you've had affairs before." Lily surprises herself with the lie, with the strength of her resolve. "The point here is that your wife recognizes some pattern in your behavior. You need to figure out what it is and change it."

"It was fifteen years ago." He whispers the confession she wishes not to hear. "It meant nothing. It wasn't like you and me. It was a fling, a stupid fling."

Lily's thoughts hum in the silence that spreads between them. How does one respond to such an admission?

"I remember how hurt she was," he whispers. "I'm such a fool."

"Stop feeling sorry for yourself." Outside her own bedroom,

Lily struggles with her bitterness as she examines the unmade bed she shares with Joseph, the blankets piled so high she worries that her husband might be waiting for her underneath. "Look." She takes a deep breath. "I'm sorry. Your wife must love you, or she wouldn't have come looking for you."

"She hates me," he says again.

Lily can tell he's exhausted, wanting to hang up or change the subject, but she's not ready to give it up. "I wouldn't be so sure," she cautions him, "but is that really the problem here?"

"What?" He sounds baffled.

"The problem is not really that your wife hates you."

Lily knows it's easier to live with hate than with meaninglessness, or maybe even love, and she wonders what will happen if Perish ever acknowledges this. She knows he loves her, but knows, too, that their affair takes place outside of dailiness, and as a result, it cannot go on forever. She still desires him, but the seasons are changing, and she wonders how long they can continue shutting their eyes on the world looming just outside, so close that it's begun to encroach. Besides, there's more to him than the confidence he used to seduce her. He has exposed a flaw in his thinking, a weakness she hadn't seen before, and she knows that unless she can master it, he will give them both away. A new, more complete image of Perish forms in her mind, and she finds herself focusing on what she missed.

Perish, I think you're going to be fine." She has agreed to meet him at their usual motel to try to calm him down. "But there's something I've been wanting to do."

"What?" he says. "Anything."

"Good," she says.

After fastening the safety latch on the door and pulling the curtain wand till the room falls into grayness, she strips off her clothes, moving deliberately in ways she knows will arouse him. Next she takes off his clothes: shirt first, the right shoe, the metal leg, which she detaches, unwrapping it and slipping it out of the padding, then pants and sock. He bends down to assist her with his underwear, but she doesn't need his help. To show that she is the expert here, she pushes him away, smiling when his butt thuds against the wall.

"I want to try this on," she says, throwing the metal leg across the bed, then joining it there. Pulling her ankle up from behind so that it's touching her butt, she begins binding her leg, wrapping it tightly into a stump. "I want to feel what it's like to be you."

He makes a move across the bed to stop her, but she puts her arm out. "I'm serious," she says firmly. "You need to let me try this."

"Let me help you, then," he says. He hops around the bed slowly as if to say, *You could stop me if you wanted; this is your game, you can change the rules at any time.* And now that she knows he's willing, she has no intention of stopping him. He encircles her hand around his cock, and she can feel his erection harden as he fastens her kneecap to the brace.

"Okay, you can fuck me," she says.

There is too much metal on the left side and not enough leg on the right to stand up straight, and she bends over the edge of the bed. "Now I'm the one missing something," she teases. "I've got your leg, and you can only have it if you—"

He enters her sharply, his hand over her mouth putting an abrupt end to speech. It's painful at first with her left leg bound uncomfortably, but she can go anywhere she wants while Perish works from behind. Far away from Perish and the semidarkness of the motel room, she finds herself unexpectedly in the garden she planted with Joseph, her husband's back pressed up against a thick tree trunk. Her father is there, too, carrying his saw, and Joseph is yelling that he's crazy, that the only reason he doesn't kill Yas is because he's lost his mind, so what would be the point? But Lily refuses to believe her father is insane. She grew up with him. She knows he's the same as he's always been, just more so, and as he begins hacking at the tree trunk, she has to admit that what he's about to do, this violent act, makes sense in its own weird way.

"Lily," Perish cuts in, urgency rippling his voice.

"Yes." She makes her way back to the room to feel him bending into her body. His abdomen pressed tightly into her back, his mouth just behind her ear, he climaxes, bringing her with him in terrifying silence.

When Lily arrives at the day-care center to take her children home, she finds Misha perched on a child-size bench. On a picnic table in front of him, he has carefully arranged a set of colorful plastic dishes with a cup and utensils beside each plate, like he's seen his mother do when setting the table for dinner. In the center is a bucket of weeds he's yanked up from the garden. He points proudly. "Flowers."

"Beautiful." She smiles.

"Come sit down." He pats the spot beside him. "Eat."

"I'd like to," she says. "But it's time to go home."

"No," he says back. "Not yet."

"Yes, now. Daddy will be waiting for us."

"No." He pours imaginary tea from a red pot and offers her a drink.

"Thank you," she says, placing her lips along the rim of the teacup and feeling how thirsty she is. "And now we really have to go."

"No." He walks away from the table. "Pizza." As he peers into the play oven, his shiny brown eyes light in anticipation. "Cheese pizza. Almost ready."

"Come on now." She is insistent. "You can play some more tomorrow."

He squints up at her. "No."

"Misha, now."

Heaving himself onto the linoleum floor, he curls his round baby's body into a ball and begins to cry.

She picks him up and cradles his body against her chest as she walks with him, an arm held out, fingers wiggling for Jessie to follow behind her. She is aware that Misha was doing something terribly important, and knows, too, that he reads her making him stop as a punishment. And for what? She wishes she could enter a world where imaginary tea can sate her thirst, a slice of pretend pizza satisfy her hunger.

On the way home, they pass corrals where baby foals, lambs, ducks, calves, and even a burro have been born, all within the last month. They play "I Spy with My Little Eye"; they play "What

Am I Thinking?" They play and talk and make up stories and watch for their favorite animals and for the new babies hiding behind trees and in the tall thick grass.

"I wish I were a horse," Jessie tells Lily wistfully.

"I want a horsie!" Misha chimes.

Lily chuckles. "I'm glad I'm *not* a horse."

"If I were a horse, you could ride me," Jessie volunteers.

"Oh, no." Lily begins to laugh.

"Why not?" Jessie says, teasing. "I'd be steady for you."

The winds come in April, shriveling fragile new leaves, plucking rose petals from their thorny stems, threatening to suck the moisture out of the children's faces so that Lily has to lather them up with lotion every night before bed. The wind, along with the sun, is how you can tell New Mexicans. They are the healthy ones with dry, weathered skin. Lily is glad her children are growing up in a rural town where local grocers call them by name and offer them special treats and kind, unhurried smiles, and even strangers wave when they drive by; glad for the wide-open spaces and the house they can afford; but she worries, too. The wind lifts last year's dead leaves along with debris from the streets: everything not secured is carried through the air to a new home. In a city where much of the land is not yet developed, dust devils spin through open fields in tight, destructive orbits. At night the wind howls. Her eyes closed in sleep, she walks into the squall, so light she is lifted off her feet and hurled into the vortex; she knows that such a course of motion will mean her end.

.   .   .

You need a vacation," Loren says again, and this time Lily
concedes. Believes that being in a different place might give
her the clarity she is no longer able to find at home. Hearing the
word *trip,* Jessie runs to her room and begins pulling open drawers, throwing clothes, books, and toys into her small suitcase.
When she is done, she gets Misha to sit on the lid because it won't
shut. He is patient and still while she works the zipper around his
legs. Animated by the sudden flurry of excitement around him,
he sings:

> *Baa-baa, black sheep, have you any wolf?*
> *Yes sir, yes sir, big bad wolf.*

Joseph arrives home from work with a headache. He does not
want to go, but away the five of them drive, leaving behind home
and dogs and trees for Loren to watch and feed and water.

The car follows the path of the river downstream. Even
though Lily can't see water, she knows it is there, hidden behind
the billowing green of cottonwoods and elms. Turning toward the
sun, she squints into the rearview mirror as Albuquerque recedes
in the distance, replaced by spotty piñon pines atop piles of sand-
stone and flattop mesas. Past Laguna pueblo and its red-rock
cliffs, past Mile High City, past Grants and Gallup, past the state
line where the New Mexico sky flattens into Arizona desert.
Even after sunset, the air is pleasant, soothing the children to
sleep as they drive with the windows down.

"I love you." Joseph slides his hand over her thigh, causing the muscles there to constrict.

She blows air out from deep within her lungs and sighs. "Any good stories at work?"

"Nothing, really."

"Oh, come on."

"A man came in the other day, a suicide."

"Oh?" She is interested in suicides.

"Gunshot to the head." He makes a pistol out of his thumb and forefinger, cocks the trigger. "Boom."

"Family?"

"A wife. He left her a note that said, *I loved you, and I loved your tits!*"

"Did you meet her?"

"She came by to talk with the social workers and collect his things."

"And . . ."

"Couldn't really tell."

"What was her response to the note?" Lily asks.

"Ah, that's a good question." Joseph grins at her. "There was some debate as to whether it would be better to let the initial shock pass first, wait a few days, or maybe not give it to her at all."

"What do you mean?" Lily is indignant. "The note belonged to her. He wrote it to her."

"Yes, and could you imagine a lewd comment on your breasts being the final word on your longest and supposedly deepest relationship?"

"Maybe she's proud of them. You can't know that."

"No." Joseph gives her a sidelong glance. "I guess you can never really know what goes on between two people. But you also have to do what you think is right. You know that."

"Whatever," Lily concedes. "I don't really know what *right* means anymore."

"That's ridiculous," Joseph snarls. "You might pretend you don't know, but you do. It's one of the things that attracted me to you. Your smug sense of what *right* is."

Yas has not moved since the trip began. He sits smiling at nothing, an empty space between the children in the back.

"Do you need to use the bathroom?" she asks him when Joseph stops for gas.

He smiles placidly.

"Come on, I'll take you."

He is still smiling.

"He's going to piss and make the car stink," Joseph observes.

"He can hear you, you know," she snaps.

"If he cared what I said, he'd get out of the car and keep walking."

"Stop," Lily warns him. "Please just stop."

As they drive on, Lily remembers the way Yas used to narrate summer trips. Early in the morning, when her thoughts were still clouded by dreams, he would recite the Latin names of wildflowers growing alongside the road; at night he identified constellations as they appeared in the quickening sky. Back then everything had a name, and every name signified something. Not like now, with the black sky announcing a million stars and all she has to go on is memory and her father's face, which does not change.

"Don't you think it's odd?" Joseph asks when they've been quiet for a while.

"What?"

"That you should be the one to care for him now."

Joseph has every reason to wonder why she's taken her father into their household. She knows it's not so much the problems associated with dementia that annoy him. It's the fact that as far as Joseph knows, she's had virtually no contact with him until now. Her husband's question is legitimate, but it irritates her. Shouldn't it be obvious to him?

"Why are you looking over here?" Lily hears her mother scolding. The lamp under the range hood shines on the crowded stovetop and illuminates perspiration beads on her forehead and a cluster of short white hairs jutting up from her crown. Standing on the stepladder, Lily marvels at the white hairs she's never noticed before. They're much shorter than the black ones, and she wonders if her mother yanks them out or if they've just recently begun to grow. "Can't you see it?" she demands, referring Lily's attention back to the task.

Turning to the high shelf, Lily pulls tentatively at the glass bowl, worried that it will tumble to the ground and ruin everything.

"Yas," her mother calls, panic ringing in her voice as Yas comes rushing in. "Honey, I could use your help."

"Who else does he have?" Lily sighs now, staring through the windshield at a cluster of lights in the distance.

"I mean, you could have put him in a nursing home, visited him on weekends. You didn't have to take him in."

"He's my father; I would never do that to him."

"Even given your history with him?"

"What's that supposed to mean?"

"Not now. I'm not talking about now that he's feeble, but before. I remember your once telling me that you hated him, that you never wanted to see him again."

"My taking care of him has nothing at all to do with how I feel about him."

"I don't understand you," Joseph says, a line that rings like a refrain.

Lily feels the truth of his words and the weight of the fact that he will probably never understand. Joseph is a man who acts because he wants to, or he doesn't act. Desire is choice. But to Lily it's more complicated than that, and darker. A black sky with a million stars that once had names, and a trait she inherited from her mother of refusing to articulate that which should be obvious. Seated beside her husband, Lily takes comfort in Perish. How his presence and even his absence evoke memory in her body, his dense weight holding her in perfect stillness while the earth wraps them in its orbit. There is no choice about this, only memory she wants never to lose. Perish, her very existence. She imagines him at home, surrounded by his wife and children. He is thinking of her, imagining her as she imagines him, or he is not thinking of her at all. The car speeds along its trajectory, and in its linear movement away from all that is dangerous and all that is safe, what is left behind ceases to exist. Her father sits behind her, his presence a persistent hum masked by the dark night, and though she does not want to, she can feel him like the pit of a plum lodged inside her throat, closer than Perish, closer than Joseph, who sits next to her, his hand still resting on her thigh.

African Queen, White Dragon, Ghurka, Immaculata, Princess Marina, delphinium.

"Why don't I have a fancy name?" Lily, as a child, once asked her father. "Why am I just *Lily*?"

"Lily is the flower of death, and of peace, a rare and delicate species."

"I want to be White Dragon Princess Immaculata," she'd said. "I want you to call me White Dragon Princess Immaculata. Don't ever call me Lily again."

Her father had smiled, a terrible, beguiling grin, so different from the way he looks at her now from the backseat. The tepid breeze and her father's insouciant grin make her shudder. She fears the diminishment of passion, which feels as inevitable to her as the fact that she is with Perish, that she could not resist him. Growing old requires finding a way to go on; he will go on with his life, unsatisfactory though it may be, go on with his wife, because for him there is no other way. But she has not lived long enough to know this yet. What she knows is that love's tragedy is not what you might think: never that one is not loved back but that one might cease to feel anything at all. And what is left behind then?

She thinks of her father, and of how he will die soon.

. . .

The night is broken by crying from the backseat. A whine that begins softly, almost imperceptibly, reminding her of the balloons she punctured with scissors after the birthday party, how they deflated slowly in her hands. They roll up windows to hear Misha waking, perhaps from a nightmare.

"It's okay, baby." Lily speaks softly to soothe him. "Shhhh."

"Misha." Joseph's voice is firmer. "Go back to sleep. We're not there yet."

"Shhhh," Lily tries again, but the crying does not stop, only becomes louder, rising like the baying of coyotes that gather in the field behind their house late at night. Unfastening her seat belt, Lily turns and reaches over the passenger seat to stroke the baby's forehead, which pierces her fingers at once with alarming heat.

"He has a fever, Joseph," she whispers, her voice trembling.

"He's probably just hot from being strapped in his car seat, and from crying."

"I don't think so," she says, pressing her cool palm against Misha's head. "He's really hot."

"I'll get off at the next stop," Joseph sighs, and Lily turns back to watch the road signs.

Lily has brought along a thermometer, which she unpacks from the dopp kit in the back. It reads 104. Misha needs Tylenol, but unfortunately she has forgotten to pack that. "What do you think is wrong with him?" she asks Joseph, panicked.

"Probably just a cold," he says.

"Does your tummy hurt, sweetheart? Your head? How about

here?" she asks, tapping lightly on Misha's earlobe. "What hurts?"

The fever is too high. Misha's eyes roll up, glassy, unresponsive to her voice, and she worries about convulsions. "We need to take him home," she decides.

"You're not serious." Joseph slams his fists dramatically into the steering wheel. "We've been driving for over four hours. We can't go back."

"Well, we can't not go back. He's too sick."

Lily rocks her limp baby in her arms. Even against Joseph's protests, it doesn't seem right to her to strap him back into his car seat. She will risk Joseph's disapproving glare to hold him against her chest, keep him safe in the only way she knows how. Nothing matters except that he is with her, because only she has the power to protect him. Misha allows himself to be calmed by her, her touch defying fever and fear. No harm will come to any of them with him tucked under her arms. She watches through the windshield, making sure Joseph stays inside the lines, hoping that the strand of lights in the distance mean a town where they can stop for Tylenol, then she turns her gaze back to Misha. "You're okay, baby," she coos. "You're going to be just fine."

Only to herself does she admit that he might not be fine. She imagines him dying in her arms the way other babies have died in their mothers' arms. Joseph has told her stories, and she tries to remind herself that these stories are not hers. She knows she must fight such thoughts and tries to push them from her head, feels for the beat of Misha's heart against her palm, the steady rise and fall of his chest as he sleeps in her lap.

"How far is the next town?" Lily demands of her husband, trying with one hand to straighten the creases out of a road map, suddenly terrified by the immense blackness that surrounds the car on all sides.

"We passed Gallup maybe two hours back." Joseph shrugs nonchalantly. "We were probably almost to Holbrook when we turned around."

"Shit," Lily says. "What should we do?"

"Keep driving." Joseph keeps his eyes focused straight ahead, and Lily wonders if his seeming unconcern is masking the same panic she feels, or whether all doctors simply lack some key emotional instinct.

"I want milk." Misha opens his eyes a half hour past Gallup to tell Lily this, to look imploringly into her eyes and beg her to nurse him. The urgency in his voice causes a tingling in her chest, and her impulse is to lift her shirt and let him suckle. *Why not? What harm could it do to try?* Then she sees Joseph looking over at her, perhaps waiting for her response. It's been a long time since she let him fondle her breasts. He knows they don't belong to Misha any longer, but he knows they don't belong to him, either. *What are you looking at?* she wants to say. *This is not any of your business.* But she realizes that of course it is. All of this is as much his business as it is hers. This is the family he's made with her: sperm and egg, not to mention the years it's taken them to get this far. Misha is *their* child, and there is no denying that this is the life they've created together.

Watching Misha's eyelids flutter, she remembers the night he was born. Early in the morning, after an exhausting afternoon and night of labor. She hadn't remembered how difficult it was to give birth, figuring that she'd done it once with Jessie and could do it again, no problem. But she'd been wrong. The contractions had sent her howling. "Do something," she'd shouted at Joseph. "Can't you do something besides just stand there?"

"Breathe," he'd told her, pressing a cold washcloth to her forehead and drawing air into his lungs, then letting it out slowly, by way of example.

"I *am* breathing," she'd hissed. "I need drugs."

"You're almost there," he'd said. "Just breathe."

She'd glared fiercely into his eyes for something to hold on to, but, finding no sign of the pain she was feeling, she'd squeezed his hand instead, feeling the sharp bones in his fingers crackle inside her palms. He'd let her hold him that way for over sixteen hours, never letting go, not even to pee or eat, and when the baby finally slid from her body, she'd dropped Joseph's hand and watched him shake his white, aching fingers, still folded in a locked embrace.

The nurse had swaddled the baby and placed him on her chest. She remembers the way he opened one eye and then the other to stare into hers, smiling when she cooed at him and he realized from her voice and smell that it had been her all along.

It has never stopped being her. She is the one he calls at night, the one who will stay up with him without sleep or complaint. It is her body that held him until he was ready to enter the world, her body that fed him and has always nurtured him. She was wrong to think that the children belong equally with Joseph.

There is nothing equal about these relationships, only a need for reciprocity that tugs at her, requiring something she cannot give.

They drive through the night, arriving home before the sun. Jessie wakes as they pull into the driveway to the familiar crunching of gravel and the garage door sighing open.

"Are we home?" Jessie wants to know.

"Yes, sweetie, we're home," Lily says.

Raising her arms over her head, Jessie yawns, then opens her eyes wide with a start. "What about our great adventure?"

"Well, we've had our great adventure," Joseph explains. Lily's head is thrown back to let him know she has no answers. Misha is sprawled across her lap, asleep.

"Weren't we going to Arizona?"

"We did go to Arizona," Joseph moans.

"But I didn't see it." Jessie begins to weep.

"Don't tease her," Lily scolds. "It's not fair."

"I'm not teasing her," Joseph says, irritated from driving through the night.

"Well, the car ride *was* the adventure." Lily, seeing no other course, follows patiently along. "Think of it that way. And now we're home."

"But I want to go to Arizona. I want to play in the river and camp under the trees. Remember? You promised."

Lily has been careful never to break a promise to Jessie. She knows how promises become held in the imagination, remembers her mother's promise never to leave her. It was nothing her mother had said, but a pact she made every night when she held and kissed Lily before bed—present every time she left and appeared again, laughing and smiling, as if by magic.

"I'll tell you what," Lily intervenes. "You help Daddy take all the things out of the back of the car, and then you think of what friend you want to invite over. Anyone you like. And when the sun comes up, Mommy will call that friend's mother and ask if she can come here for a sleepover. Then you and your friend can camp in the backyard under the stars."

"Can the dogs sleep in the tent with us?"

"Yes. All of them, if you'd like."

"Hooray," Jessie yells, causing Misha to startle. "You're the best mommy in the whole world. This is going to be so fun!"

The mother is perfect. Her mother was perfect. Her daughter is perfect. The mother dissolves to take her place among the stars, leaving the daughter, her perfect image, behind.

What was once perfection is left behind.

Misha's fever refuses to abate. For three days it drops off only to rise again. The pediatrician offers a diagnosis: either a viral or a bacterial infection, which means it could be anything. But first Misha turns his head from side to side so that the doctor can look inside each of his ears, then raises his shirt with both hands, exposing his round belly to be probed and poked in a way that makes Lily marvel at how trusting he is, how innocent. Finally he accepts a wooden tongue depressor, a bribe, and opens his mouth wide only to gag when the long cotton swab scratches the back of his throat.

"How old is this kid?" the doctor asks.

"How old are you, Misha?" Lily prompts.

"I'm *five*," he says proudly, his sister's age.

Lily smiles. "He's two, just two last month."

"You just might be five," the doctor says, impressed, "except that you're a little short for five."

Insulted, Misha roars his lion's roar, baring his teeth and extending his chubby fingers like claws, and Lily feels the betrayal of having explained to him beforehand how he should cooperate because the doctor was going to help make his fever go away, this same doctor who seems not to understand, or even much like, children.

"So can you tell me where it hurts?" the doctor asks.

"I'm fine." Misha beams, folding his arms protectively over his naked abdomen. "I'm not sick."

Aside from the fever, there are no symptoms other than lethargy, his body weary from the extreme heat it is generating in an attempt to kill off infection. He seems not to mind any discomfort as long as Lily will hold him, carry him around the house the way she used to do for whole days at a time, while fixing dinner and tidying; she even helps Jessie brush her teeth with him in her arms. At naptime and bedtime he clings even more fiercely, wrapping his arms around her neck or patting the bed beside him. "Lie down, Mommy," he pleads. "Stay here."

This shouldn't bother her; it's something she did for years, lying on her side next to Jessie and then Misha while they drifted to sleep, warm milk from her body softening their dreams, but it's been months since he was weaned, and in that time he's learned to go to sleep without her. She doesn't want to go back on the progress he's made. But maybe it's not him she's worried about. She repeats the same stories over and over, hoping they will help him fall asleep the way they almost put her to sleep while telling them. Success means she can leave his bed, and she waits beside him, wondering how she mustered the fortitude to make it through the last five years and why every minute spent in his bed feels like too long.

Even in sleep he calls her to him, his grip on her tightening when she tries to slip away. She knows she's not spoiling him, that sometimes it's necessary to go backward in order to move forward. She does not want to stay with him, but stroking his curls, damp with fever, away from his fat baby cheeks, it does not occur to her that she has a choice. Late into the night she soothes him, patiently whispering stories of foxes and rabbits and their adventures through an enchanted forest. She knows the rule: there must always be foxes and rabbits.

At the end of the third night, when Lily moves from his bed into her own, she finds Joseph waiting for her. He turns toward her and his hands slide up under her nightgown; his mouth finds her mouth, and he seems to take pleasure in the heat of her body against his. This is something she's tried to avoid. Tried to enter the room quietly and to slip without sound between the sheets. She wants to tell him to stop, but she is afraid she won't say that;

afraid that she will speak Perish's name if she tries to say anything, or that her words will come out too harshly or loud. Too tired to find the right words, she lies still beneath him, praying for the moment he will roll away. Sleep will come soon, she reassures herself, but after he has left her body, an ache she can't identify fills her core, spreading its crooked fingers until no part of her is untouched by pain. No longer able to keep silent, she begins to weep.

"What's wrong, Lily?" he whispers.

He has heard her, though that is not what she intended. She wished to cry silently, and only long enough to let go of the ache, but she has failed, and his questioning points to her failure, making her sobs come louder and more forcefully.

"I'm tired," she offers at last, the one confession she can possibly make. "I'm exhausted, and I feel like I need to sleep for a year."

"Maybe I can take a few days off and help you."

"No!" she yells back, irrational. "I need at least a year to catch up. I've lost too much. I'm way too tired.

"Besides," she adds, calmer, "I seem to be having a crisis."

Rolling his eyes, Joseph turns away. "Fine," he says. "Maybe I'll have one with you."

I've missed you enormously," Perish tells her when she goes to visit him at his office. Misha's fever has finally broken.

"It's good to see you" is all she'll say.

"I liked what you did the last time I saw you."

She smiles. "I'm glad."

"I was afraid you weren't happy with me. You stayed away for so long."

She wants to weep, to tell him how utterly difficult the last days have been, but she stares across his desk, somberly assessing the office where she has come so often.

"Come here," he says. He tells her about his fantasies of their being together here, where it would be so easy to be seen by anyone passing underneath the low windows, or heard on the other side of the thin wall.

She wants to tell him he's crazy, but she scoots back her chair and goes to him. "We could get caught, you know."

"I don't care anymore," he says, wrapping her in his arms. "I've missed you too much."

"You should care." A breeze drifts through the open window, mixing with the smell of dirty carpet, worn from years of being walked on. She wiggles free from his arms, pulls a heavy book from the shelves that line the wall behind him, and begins reading titles: "*Strangers from a Different Shore, Asian Immigration in the Early Twentieth Century, Executive Order 9066: The Internment of 110,000 Japanese Americans.* How does it feel to be an expert?" she wants to know.

He tries to take the heavy book from her, but she clamps it against her chest. "Give me a critical assessment of the impact of the internment on Japanese-Americans during the Second World War," she says. "As a historian and a scholar."

"What are you talking about?" he demands, and she notes how quickly his mood has shifted from amorous to fed up.

"I'm serious," she says. "It's a fact of our lives; you should know that."

"What?"

"What we don't talk about it, what your wife and my husband can't get inside."

"I'm not following you. Please come here," he says.

He reaches for her, and the space he describes with his out-stretched arms looks like an enormous hole she might fall into if she's not careful. Without thinking, she tosses the book she's been clutching into the hole. The binding thuds against his right foot, and the book crackles open between them.

"Ouch," he cries, looking down indignantly. "You've damaged an expensive book."

It was an accident, a failed experiment for which she should apologize—she could have hurt him—but in a sudden move, he grabs her and locks her against his chest. Now he's laughing, and his laughter hurts her ears. She can see that he cares only about seducing her, but she is determined to make the rules for what will happen in his office this afternoon. Snatching a new book from his shelf, she rips out a page and stuffs it into his mouth.

He spits it out and wrestles the book from her grasp, but there are plenty more books on the shelf, and with one sweep of her arm, they all come tumbling down. "You infuriate me," she says, shoving him to the floor and burying him under a pile of books.

"Cut it out," he protests, flailing his arms to protect his face and groin from sharp corners.

"No." She is the master of this interlude; only she can say

when it will end. She brings down a second row of books, but she can't stop there. She buries him under his books until no part of him is exposed, and then she clears a space big enough to work through. Loosening his belt and unzipping his trousers, she digs inside his underwear and takes his penis in her hands, surprised to find it erect. She's rough with him, clamping his erection between her teeth, sucking him, then pulling back right before he climaxes, sucking again, working him until his semen shoots into the air, damaging his precious books forever.

When the moans beneath the books subside, Lily collapses on top of the pile. With her eyes closed, she lets herself be drawn in by the fresh smell of Perish's semen, mixed with the even stronger odor of old paper, glue, and ink.

"You know, my mother would have loved you," she says, as if to lay words over what just happened.

"I want you again," he murmurs, shifting beneath her, knocking away some of the books between them.

"My mother was alive when I went away to college," she says, running her fingers across a book binding. "I never bothered to introduce her to anyone I dated because I knew she wouldn't have liked my boyfriends. I *know* she wouldn't approve of my husband. But she would have loved you, because you're Japanese."

"Japanese are skittish about death." Perish emerges, resting his head on the cover of a book.

"Whatever." Lily is perturbed by his comment, which she has not invited. "But she would have loved you."

"No—" Perish starts to say.

"You're smart, educated, handsome," Lily muses. "So is Joseph"—she glances his way—"but you would have understood my mother the way Joseph has never understood me. Joseph never met her, but they wouldn't have gotten along. I've never been at peace, knowing that."

"I want to feel what it's like to be you." He watches her, tilting his head at the same angle as hers. He uses her words back on her until she climbs on top of him, her body straddling his in a forceful rhythm.

W hat do you want?" Joseph asks unexpectedly when she arrives home late with the children. "Because it's obviously not me."

Taken aback, Lily stands at the window in their bedroom, looking for the green cherries she noticed hanging from the tree the other day. She knows they are there, inches from the window, but she can't quite see out. "I want another life," she says, and she begins to cry.

"What does that mean?" he asks. "Do you want a divorce?"

"No," she says. "Just another life. It's hard to explain to you how really tired I am. I have my work, which has fallen way behind; I have Misha who's barely well, and Jessie's demands. And then there are yours. I'm not sure I can pull it off anymore—any of it."

She, who has always been sure of her ability to pull off anything she puts her mind to, remembers the gleam that once lit her father's eyes when he set out to teach her about flowers.

Lily; Lilium.

He grew every variety of lily imaginable, taught her first to admire them: *Black Dragon, Pink Perfection, Madonna.* And then to identify them: *Lilium regale, pyrenaicum, candidum, formosanum.*

At five, Jessie's age, she dreamed of the sleek, cylindrical calla lily, its delicate shape and bountiful colors giving way to long, arrow-shaped leaves in the damp hugeness of the greenhouse where the flowers were kept in moist clay pots, all in a row. Saw her father with garden shears in hand, skulking into her room, where she lay with her back to him, the rank smell of fertilizer and sudden heat announcing his presence. *Lilium regale, pyrenaicum, candidum, formosanum.*

Say them. Lily.

When potting, make sure you don't destroy the root system. Use plenty of rich soil. Soak generously. Prune by clipping away the dead growth. Water at the base, never the petals. These rules, as simple to her now as following instructions on a box of cake mix, had sent her head spinning. *How do you know if you're destroying the root system? How much water do plants need? How can you tell when a leaf is dead, and why don't petals like getting wet?* Her father had dismissed her questions, making her believe that his knowledge was arcane, rather than too rudimentary to merit explanation. On her birthday, he gave her one plant to start with, a small, bulbous cactus that he claimed was hearty and could withstand New York winters and neglect. Alone in her room, she'd watered the cactus, leaving her bed in the middle of the night to poke her finger into the sandy soil and check for dampness in case she'd forgotten, though she never did. In the middle of the night, if necessary, she'd trail into the bathroom for a cup of water and pour it tenderly into the soil, peering to find enough light in the darkness: she would not let the plant dry out. During the day, she sang and talked to the cactus, praying for flowers and rapid growth, until her father appeared in her room one day to issue a decree: "You've killed it!"

Mortified, Lily rushed to the small pot, which she had set beneath her desk lamp for extra light. She wanted to tell her father that he was wrong. The plant was alive; she knew it was because she'd only just looked, but all that came was a small shrug as she struggled to locate the place within herself that had understood even before her father's pronouncement that the plant was dead. It had been dying for weeks, beyond rescue by a five-year-old's nurturing. No amount of water, soil amendments, or artificial light to supplement the short winter days would bring it back.

"You've leeched vital nutrients from the soil with too much water, and you've burned the crown with this incandescent bulb. It's amazing you didn't start a fire." Her father leaned over her desk, close enough that she could feel his breath against her shoulders, his authority pushing up against her innocent belief that she was doing a good thing. She knew she'd made a serious mistake; it was one any child could make, but the results made her want to cry.

I didn't mean to... she'd been about to say, but instead, anger made her shaking hand slam into the long spines of the dead plant, and then the tears came. It hurt to feel the prickles embedded in her palm, to learn about the toxins carried through the needles as they were removed, one sharp prick after another, to learn how the poison that protected the cactus made your hand swell up in pain.

That night her father let himself in without knocking, his eyes shifting from her body curled on the bed to the cactus that still sat on her desk, because how could she throw it away? Even a dead thing that has no use must be properly handled. She knew this, though she had not yet decided what to do. It would sit in her room untended, daily losing shape, until it shriveled and became light as driftwood and pale as stone. Late at night, Yas hovered over her bed with a good-night kiss. *Black Dragon, Pink Perfection, Madonna, Lilium regale, pyrenaicum, candidum, formosanum.*

"Next time you will know better," he whispered after shutting out the light. "Remember that I am trying to teach you about life; there are many things you have to learn."

She could not respond to his remonstrance, angry to know already the lesson he would never learn because he refused to prize her love over the dead cactus. But as it turned out, the cactus was not dead. Early in the spring, the withered plant turned from gray to green, and tiny yellow flowers appeared between the barbs. Now, seeing his face frozen like the surface of water, she believes she can see something she might have missed then: even though he is hopelessly lost inside his fragile mind and dying body, she cannot let him go. She still needs to call him back.

. . .

But maybe her recollection of the past is not what happened at all. What if the cactus was only a plant, and what if there was no sense to be made, or what if the sense she has made no longer serves her? Whatever understanding is to be gained will have to come from her. It is up to her to make sense with him, to make sense for him. What she understood then was that he hated her, or worse yet, that her love of him meant nothing. But what if she was wrong?

Perish is insatiable: he wants to know about Joseph, her children, her father, the accident that killed her mother.

She will not divulge information about her life with her husband, her children, her father—such talk would require coming to conclusions. But her job has trained her well to discuss the past. And who can resist the tug of history?

"It was a clear night." She sees, as she has countless times before, stars lighting the road like an outstretched arm pointing the way home. "He flipped the car into an embankment. She was crushed. He walked away."

Lily dares not ask about Perish's wife or children, but she begs him to tell her about the loss of his leg.

"I had a motorcycle," he tells her. "Before my children, but not before my wife.

"My wife." He pauses, eyes Lily as if to assess her response to words not yet spoken. "My beautiful wife, whom I once loved more than all the world. She hated the motorcycle. To her it was dangerous and unreliable. But to me it was affordable. And dangerous. I'd take it out on weekends. People thought I was crazy to want to leave my beautiful wife behind. But it's not easy to live with perfection. I might have been beautiful once, but I have never been perfect. I had scars, stories she'd never once asked to hear, until one day I came home broken."

He stares hopelessly past his left kneecap, but listening to him, Lily does not feel despair. She thinks she can almost see a leg forming there in the void.

"She never cried," he sighs. "As if she'd known all along. As if such a thing could be known.

"'I'm pregnant,' she told me the same night. Like an accusation. Like a myth. As if the two events were somehow conjoined. My arriving home broken, and the part of me that had entered her whole. As if those things were the same."

"That's amazing," Lily muses. "One thing gone and another already being dreamed up out of the void."

"By the way," he says, "it's not his fault."

"What?" she demands, unable to make the leap from one story to the next. "Not *whose* fault?"

"That he walked away. How could that be his fault?"

Suddenly she gets it. But how could he know enough to assess blame? "He *killed* her," she says.

"No." He shakes his head sadly. "She killed him. She is alive in her perfect daughter—immortal. But he's dead, already dead, though he doesn't suspect it. One thing happened when another seemed more likely.

"Trust me," he tells her. "I'm old enough to know."

"What do you know?" She presses fingers into her temples, feeling light-headed and slightly addled by his talk.

"I cannot equal your perfection," he tells her. "But I can love you because of your flaw."

"What's my flaw?"

"I am."

The mirror is perfect, never refusing to reflect a thing, never discriminating between ugly or beautiful. Misha stares into the mirror beside Lily as she watches on, making the children late for bedtime stories. After reading theirs, she goes to Yas's room and reads him one, too.

"Trees are nice," his favorite book begins. "They fill up the sky.

"A tree is nice for a house to be near. The tree shades the house and keeps it cool. . . . The tree holds off the wind and keeps the wind from blowing the roof off the house sometimes.

"That's why we don't cut down trees." She adds this epilogue before shutting the book, believing that he is lost in his private, unhearing world.

"A dead tree needs to be cut down," he says, surprising her. "There are many good reasons to cut down a tree."

He may not remember the names of her children or recognize the house he inhabits, but he still knows about trees, and now she thinks she might understand that perhaps he really was right in the knowledge his experience has given him. Look at the world, contained in the life of a tree, and maybe he is right. Defeat means not only a lost tree but a lost life as well. Defeat is shutting down because life is too much to bear.

She's sad all the time. She returns with Perish to his house in the mountains, but all the excitement she felt before has left her. She doesn't want to make love. She unties the decorative curtains so that she can shut out the light, and she lies in his bed with her clothes still on, her eyes closed, allowing him to stroke her hair in the dark.

"I'm sorry," she says.

"Don't be," he says. "Why are you always saying you're sorry?"

"Enormous guilt." She shrugs.

Her eyes are open now, but his have closed, and she thinks he's falling asleep when she hears his voice. " 'There was earth inside her, and she dug,' " he whispers next to her ear.

"What?" she says, not sure she's heard anything at all.

"You remind me of a poem," he says, "lines that have been in my head since the day I met you."

"Tell me," she says, propping herself on her elbows.

" 'There was earth inside her, and she dug,' " he begins. "Wait, I think I'm changing it a little.

"Hold on," he says, pushing himself off the bed and hopping away. He returns with a book of poems, and she can feel her heart race as he opens it and begins leafing through the well-worn pages. "Paul Celan," he says. "I love Paul Celan."

"Good," she says. "So do I." And she looks over his shoulder as he reads.

I'm afraid I can't work with what you're giving me," Joseph says at last, a response more to the massive silence that has wedged its way between them than to her. "It's not enough. I don't know what you need."

"I don't know, either," she says.

"Well, if you figure it out, you know I'll be happy to help you, to do anything I can to help."

"I want to be understood without having to ask for under-standing," she says.

"I don't think it's ever possible to have that."

Joseph swears beyond all hope that such a state of intimacy cannot exist, even calls it blackmail. But she knows that it does. To want is to lack, and desire is the only emotion powerful enough to make a thing real. Desire is what makes her feel alive. Perish makes her feel alive, believes in the longing that draws them together, and in doing so offers her something that is not happiness but existence in the earth's timeless hum.

Lily's mother wanted only her happiness, and her soul. Told her and still speaks promises that Lily has kept and memo-rized: "You are that indispensable part of me that holds me to the earth, keeps me alive. You are the thing that is more necessary than air or food, the one thing I cannot do without."

There is no reason for her death, and yet death comes for her. *Imagine it. A windy night late in fall. No clouds, no fog or rain obscuring the road, a flat stretch lit by a half-moon and stars extending like an arm pointed toward home.* What choice does Lily have but to believe in the mystery that she has created?

Maybe you're right," she tells Joseph, lying because she is angry with him.

"I know I'm right," Joseph tells her, pulling her close, his cock stiffening as his mouth sinks over her breasts. She does not want him, but he is careful not to notice. She makes the rules and he plays by them, refusing to see. Were he to look, he would know about Perish, and then he would have to go back to the beginning, and she will not let him go there. Joseph plays because he wants to, taunting her with his tongue, spreading her open like a flag, her body flared and quivering beneath him. She does not want him, but she relents, no longer wishing to avoid what is real; let him be right, inside the locked room where they share a bed, in their adobe home with its hushed walls that keep her safe. There is nowhere for her to go and her body moves powerfully beneath him, finding itself in motion.

The nighthawks have arrived. She hears them late at night outside the open window, mocking the coyotes, swooping down to steal food before ascending, enormous white wings flapping skyward like a wraith or a portent. Dreams come in their wake like writing made invisible by the night sky. A vaporous trail falling into her open hands, and she reads it. Even though it is not in any language she has ever seen, she has always been good at interpreting signs. They come nightly now, incrementally, the way all true knowledge does. She falls asleep believing she is wide awake; she has nightmares until one morning she wakes up certain she's living all the dreams she once had. She is no longer asleep, and there is no new dream in sight.

Three

re you sleeping with your husband?" Perish's voice cracks over the phone, and she cannot decide whether it's trepidation she hears or static caused by a faulty wire. It is a question she has thoughtfully tried to avoid without being deceptive, to cast aside what's given and live apart from it, shielded from the world in her desire of him.

"I could ask the same of you," she says, stalling, already knowing the answer.

"I'm not sleeping with my wife. I'd tell you if I were."

"I'm happy to hear that," she says. "I don't think I could stand it if you were."

"How about you. You didn't answer my question."

"Well, yes. I am." Words rush from her lips and catch in the air, and she stares into the space they create. She tries to imagine him, standing or sitting down, talking to her from a house she's never seen. The distance between them feels enormous, irreconcilable, as she tries desperately to locate him. She knows he needs more details than she has given him, yet what else can she possibly say?

She could tell him how this morning she thought only of him. When Jessie procrastinated in front of her jewelry box and Misha could not decide which shoes to wear, Lily smiled and let them take their time, considering how, months before, she had wondered whether Perish could be real, and if so, why it had taken her this long to be able to *see* him. His arms catching her in midair and turning her in slow circles, stripping off her clothes and fucking her with abandon before settling down to lie with her, to know something indescribably pleasurable and secret.

Then, walking into the garage, Jessie had shut the door behind them and everything had changed. Lily, hearing the lock click, dove backward, slamming her palm into the solid oak door. "No!"

The keys lay on the kitchen table, appearing like an idea that came to mind the moment the door had slammed—the shiny silver feather catching the light, no way to get to it in time. It had been pandemonium after that, Lily with two children trailing behind like ducklings, stopping first at the hiding spot for the spare key, which, it turned out, had not been returned after the last time she locked herself out, then circling the house for an open window by which to enter. The one they'd found was the one Lily suspected might be open, the small rectangular window over the tub, held three quarters shut by a wooden dowel. Lily couldn't squeeze even her head through the tiny space, though she tried. "Let me try, Mommy," Jessie said with her usual confidence. Lily imagined her daughter lowering herself through the window, grabbing the keys from the kitchen table, and skipping out the garage door to rescue them all. But Jessie did not fit, either. "I guess we'll have to go to the neighbor's and call Daddy," she said, dragging her feet as she walked away in a dramatic show of disgust.

"No, wait!" Lily called after her. "We don't need Daddy. Let's just think for a minute first, okay?" To call Joseph would mean pulling him from morning report, an event he should not miss, and in turn incurring his anger. But more importantly, the long wait would mean missing Perish at the spot where they'd agreed to meet.

"I have an idea." She let her eyes twinkle down at her son. "I bet Misha can fit through the window. I bet he can do it. Think you can do it, Misha?" she asked, smiling and nodding vigorously at her baby to signal the correct answer.

"No," Misha said firmly, but that was his response to most everything, and Lily knew not to be so easily deterred.

"Do you know what Mommy is asking?"

"No," he said again, this time clenching his fists at his sides.

Lily called her daughter back to help, knowing that Jessie could convince him of things in crucial moments when no one else could. "Do you think Misha could get Mommy's keys?"

Jessie shrugged.

"Well, you're right, I suppose. Maybe he's too small. Maybe someday when he's as grown up as you. Right, Jessie?"

"Okay." Misha began nodding, his pride wounded. "I can."

"Great," said Lily. "Good."

Misha raised his arms to be hoisted through the window, but

Lily, squatting in the dirt, sat him on her lap first. "Now, here's what I want you to do," she began, worried as he picked blades of grass from the bottoms of his shoes. "Are you listening, Misha?"

Misha nodded, and Lily positioned her face close to his ear. "Mommy and Jessie are going to lift you up like Mommy lifted Jessie before. Only you're going to go into the house all by yourself, like a really big boy, and you're going to go to the kitchen table and get Mommy's keys, and then you're going to go to the door that leads out to the garage and open it, and Jessie and Mommy will be standing right there waiting for you. Okay?"

Misha only nodded, still picking at his shoes.

It was not a foolproof plan, perhaps it was even a foolish one, but Lily lifted him, grabbing hold of his hands to lower him into the bathtub, where he dropped into a ball and immediately began to scream. "Misha," Lily called, worried that he had dislocated one of his arms on the way down. "What's wrong, baby? Tell Mommy, please."

But it was no good. Lily knew that whatever had gone wrong, she would have to wait until the tears subsided. She looked down at Jessie, who stood beside her tapping a foot, causing puffs of dirt to rise in the hot morning air. Jessie had already learned to act cool, pretending to dismiss the panic Lily knew she was feeling over Misha's tears. "He's okay, I think," she told Jessie.

"Then why is he crying?" Jessie asked accusingly.

"I don't know. But I think he's okay."

"Maybe he's stuck," Jessie offered, and then it occurred to Lily: what she had not anticipated was the fear she had bred into her baby about tubs. He was never, *never* to get into the tub by

himself. Tubs were dangerous. Tubs were where two-year-olds drowned. And now Misha was in the tub alone, and frightened, and she could do nothing.

"Misha." She spoke softly. "I know you're in there by yourself, and that's probably very scary, but there's no water in the bathtub, and Mommy is right here watching you."

The sobs became softer; she'd guessed right.

"Mommy's here, Misha," she called gently. "Now, let's see if you can stand up all by yourself and climb over the edge of the tub and go open the door."

"What's he doing now?" Jessie asked when the moment of silence seemed to linger.

"He's doing just fine; you're doing great, Misha. See, I knew you could do this." Then Lily, pulling Jessie behind her, darted around the corner of the house to observe through windows as Misha made his way to the kitchen table and found the keys.

"Yay," Lily called. "Hooray for Misha."

"Yippee," Jessie cheered him on, enthused that somehow the delay had turned into a celebration.

Running into the garage, they waited for Misha's short legs to catch up to their longer ones. "What are you doing in there now?" Lily called through the door, but there was no response.

"Misha," she tried again. "Come open the door." For a full minute she did not move. Should she stay where she was to greet him like she'd said she would, or go back around the house to peer in the window? "You stay here," she declared at last, tousling Jessie's hair. "I'll go look in the window and find out what's taking him so long."

"Right," Jessie said, the excitement of moments before obviously having left her.

"It won't take long," Lily assured her daughter before returning to the kitchen window, only to spot Misha seated atop the counter, helping himself to a dish of M&M's. It was funny, she had to admit it, but she couldn't laugh. "Misha," she called through the window, careful to speak softly and not to bang on the pane. The last thing she wanted was to startle him and make him lose his balance. "Misha, sweetie. Put the M&M's down and come open the door for Mommy and Jessie like we talked about. Remember?"

"Two more." He held out yellow and green palms so she could see.

"No more," Lily called back. "I'm going to start counting, and by the time I reach three, I want you off that counter and at the door like you said. One, two . . ."

Interrupted by the appearance of Jessie tugging at her pant leg, she never got to three. "I thought I told you to wait in the garage," she said to Jessie, irritated.

Jessie turned to leave, her head lowered and shoulders slouched in a way that made Lily recant. "What?" she called to her daughter's back.

"Nothing." Jessie kept walking.

"I'm sorry," Lily called. "Please come back and tell me."

"We should get Grandpa Yas to open the door," Jessie mumbled.

"My goodness, you're brilliant!" Lily exclaimed. "Why didn't I think of that?"

Leaving Misha balanced precariously on the countertop, the two ran hand in hand once more around the house. A haze covered the guest room window. Lily assumed it was the glare cast by the morning sun, then noted the smudge her hand had made when she pulled it away. "I can't see anything. Can you see?" she asked Jessie.

"He's right"—Jessie paused—"there. There he is." She pointed to the bed, where Yas lay in his underwear, without even a sheet covering him. "I think he's dead," she said.

"He's not dead." Lily clucked, and she blamed Joseph for making death an everyday possibility in their household. "Dad!" She thrummed her fingernails against the glass, but still he didn't move. "I don't *think* he's dead."

"Grandpa Yas!" Jessie shrieked at the top of her lungs.

Yas's head began to move, slowly at first and then more purposefully after his hand had located his eyeglasses on the nightstand.

Why hadn't Lily thought of her father in the first place? This was going to be simple. "Hi," they all mouthed, smiling and waving their recognition.

"Open the window," Lily called, motioning with her hands. "We're locked out."

Yas cupped his hand behind his ear. The glass was thick, and his hearing wasn't particularly good these days. Lily could see his mouth moving and imagined him saying, *I can't hear you.*

No kidding, she thought, staring down at her watch. Then her mind flashed back to Misha, perched on the kitchen counter—at least she hoped he was still up there. For all she knew, he had fallen and lay unconscious or even—. She could have gone one step further in berating herself for this preposterous situation, so clearly her fault, but her intense anger found an outlet instead in her father. "Go open the door, dammit!"

She yelled and pointed down the hall until Jessie grasped her elbow. "It's okay, Mom," she said. "Stop."

Lily looked down at her daughter, who smiled benevolently at Yas, raising her cupped hand and waving a signal that said, gently, *Come.*

She stared from her daughter to her father, who rose from his bed, made his way to where they stood, and, after fumbling with the lock, lifted the window high enough for Lily to slide through the opening. "Bravo," she called back to Jessie. You are so good. *Too* good!"

Misha stood just inside the door, waving the keys, his prize, but by that time Lily was shaken and irritable. "Thank you, Misha," she said curtly, pulling him up for a brief hug before strapping him into his car seat.

"May I have my keys now?" Lily held her hand out, palm upturned, smiling.

"No," he balked, clutching them between his fingers like spokes. "My keys."

"Misha," Lily sighed, exasperated. "There's no time for this. I need my keys to drive the car. You know that."

"Mine," he said, settling on the shiny silver feather and stroking it with a bent finger.

"I'll make you a deal," Lily told him. "That's Mommy's special feather. But if you give me my keys, I'll take that feather off the ring so that you can play with it while I drive."

. . .

Lily uses her grip on the steering wheel to steady her hands. She has tapped all her energy reserves to get this far into the day, but it isn't hunger or fatigue causing her to tremble. She thinks she might still make it on time to meet Perish, and she knows as well that she's gone too far. What could she possibly have been thinking, dropping her two-year-old through the high window, and into the bathtub at that! And poor Jessie, unassuming witness to her lunacy. She guesses that mothers have been labeled unfit for far less serious mistakes.

Racing down the highway, it's not the road in front of her that holds her attention. In between thoughts of Perish, she sees her father balancing on the end of his bed in his underwear, a stupid smile lighting his face. Soon, she knows, she'll have to face the fact that it's irresponsible of her to leave him home by himself, or even to have him around the children. It's not fair to them. He could cause a fire, hurt himself, make a costly mistake that could even *kill* somebody. Even so, at the moment there are more immediate concerns.

Once they have arrived her fingers work busily to remove Misha from his seat. "Where's the feather?" she asks. His round eyes brim with amusement, the same shiny brown eyes that always make her feel happy.

He shrugs. "Gone."

"Not funny," she says with her hand out. "Where is it?"

"He threw it out the window," Jessie cuts in.

"You tossed Mommy's special feather out the window?" Lily cries. "Why?"

He shrugs again.

"Maybe he thought it was like a bird's feather or something," Jessie offers.

Lily doesn't know what to say. Retracing the morning drive, she imagines the feather lying somewhere along I-25, the wind blowing against their faces as she whispers Perish's name, hoping she might still make it to their meeting place—the feather leaving Misha's hands, catching in the air and landing, now flattened by tire treads.

She does not see Perish; the phone in her office is ringing when she rushes in after having driven a circle around their motel.

"I'm sorry," she says again, instead of offering him the retraction she knows he craves. She does not say, *Don't worry, because sex with my husband is awful.* She does not say, *I won't do it again.* She does not lie, though out of allegiance to whom, she does not know. "I lost something very important to me this morning," she says, distracted.

"Oh?" He, too, clearly wishes to move away from the subject at hand. "What did you lose?"

"Nothing," she says. "A feather. A gift from Joseph the year he and I were married."

She wants to tell him the story, but she cannot think of a way to begin. Should she talk about her husband and the luck the feather sealed between them? Talk about how, years before, the feather signaled his arrival in her life? And what can it mean that it's gone, not in any way she'd ever imagined losing it, but gone nonetheless.

"I still want to make love to you," he whispers into the phone.

"Okay." She feels his pain as her own, a queasiness that rises from her gut, because she has hurt him.

"Is there enough time?" he asks.

"Yes," she lies. There is no time, not really. Her class is scheduled to begin in an hour, but she doesn't want to resist him.

They meet at the Four Winds like two strangers. She stays in her car, watching in the rearview mirror as he walks to the office to check them in. Their hands lock as they climb the worn-out stairs, an ugly iron banister leading the way to the room on the second floor. Once inside, they do what they always do: he bolts the door behind them, she goes to draw the curtains. But before shutting them in, she stares out the window at the rough glare of concrete below, where trucks fit together like strange puzzle pieces. The massive boxes of silver steel huddle as if frozen in some graceless mating ritual. She might never have noticed them were it not for Perish and the rooms they inhabit together, overlooking the truck stop. She has seen them countless times, so the sight of them is as engrained in her as the length of muscle beneath Perish's slack skin, and she wonders if, careening into her own death, she will see the trucks like the tunnel her mother passed through, some sort of purgatory.

"Do you still desire me?" he asks when he turns from the door to find her still gazing out at the lot. He approaches her from behind, spinning her in slow circles, then folding his body into hers, lifting her hair to kiss her neck as he slides the straps of her sundress over her shoulders, past her elbows.

"Yes," she says, unbuttoning his shirt, then his jeans, sliding them from his waist and forcing them to the floor with her foot.

He is everywhere. She inhales his scent, which fills the air between them, turning heat instantly to dampness. He collects her in his arms, the invisible hairs on her neck and back rising to meet his touch. Her limbs join his in motion as fluid and ceaseless as a beating heart.

"You remind me of a bird," he whispers. "Your wings are always fluttering, making the air around you take notice.

"You remind me of a small, beautiful bird."

She closes her eyes and envisions the shadows beneath them becoming bird wings, and the bird ascending to circle the dark room, its wide motions getting smaller and more intricate, like liquid emptying itself from a funnel, until it disappears into her body and lodges inside her chest. A moan like something dying rises and escapes from her lips.

"Do you love me?"

Her heart skips a beat, or is it footsteps on the stairs? She is conscious of never having told him she loves him. It's been so important to keep love separate from desire. Love is what she reserves for her children, and sometimes for her husband. She desires Perish, does not love him. *"Yes,"* she tells him, not recognizing the sound of her own pain. Wrapping her legs around his torso, she pulls him deeply into her, and his body fills with movement the space in her held just for him; then, finding her center, he holds her—his arms encircling her, his body perfectly still.

When the body lies motionless, she knows, the force of gravity is imperceptible to the eye, but she imagines the earth spinning powerfully around the sun. The bird has been set free inside her, and it beats its wings against her chest, colliding with bone and pliant but impenetrable layers of skin, pounding against the walls of her body for escape.

They make love again and again, stopping only briefly before coming together once more. They make love until she lifts herself from the bed feeling bruised and dizzy.

"I need a shower," she tells him, but after closing herself in the bathroom and sitting on the edge of the tub, she lets the spray brush her face, knowing she won't get in. Looking down between her legs, she sees traces of their lovemaking evident in the harsh overhead light. Sweet and procreant fluids, the very substance of their lives, sticky and shimmering. Sitting on the edge of the white tub, water screaming down from above, she knows for the first time that she cannot possibly return home and, in the same instant, knows she must leave. The water still running, she returns to the dark room, certain she cannot stay one minute longer.

"I need to leave," she says behind her, using the chest of drawers to steady her weight while she pulls her sundress over her head, stumbles into her sandals, and, grabbing her panties, shoves them into the gaping mouth of her handbag. "I'm late for class." She sees his naked body only as a dark spot in the middle of white sheets, lit by questioning eyes. "And I'm not feeling well."

As she walks to her car, her mind locks on the feather and its mysterious but ultimately senseless disappearance. *It's over now,* she tells herself, and a rush overtakes her, making her believe that her feet no longer touch the ground. It is like walking on air, like spinning circles through clouds until her body, lifted into the wind on a sudden swell, drops down on the pavement.

She is an accomplice to a murder. In darkness in the backseat of a car in a narrow alley, someone gets killed. Perish is the murderer. He sits in the front seat, and she knows she must flee. Into the crowded streets of Manhattan, where no one notices the bloodstains on her clothing. It is a stormy orange sunset, and they are all watching the sky. Arriving at a brownstone she lived in a long time ago, she takes the elevator up to the green bathroom. She must wash the bloodstains out of her dress, but she is distracted by her reflection in the mirror over the sink. Her hair and eyes look wild, her skin glistens, electric; it is an image she would like to gaze at longer. But she must not look. There is a party for her. Everyone from the university is there. No one speaks to her. They all stare, and no one turns away. That is how she knows they all know. She is so beautiful, dressed in a slinky, strappy, pink beaded gown and matching heels. This is her send-off. The bloodstains, though invisible, have been detected. She is going to prison. Perish is at the party, but they do not speak; they only cast glances at each other from across the room. The room becomes a diner where she joins him, taking a seat across from him in a cracked red vinyl booth that seats four.

"Look," he says, handing her a menu. He's scratched on the back *Rules for Conduct*. *"Beware, the doorman knows,"* the first line reads.

There are other items on the list, but she refuses to look at them. She is going to prison for a murder he's committed, though not intentionally, and he is handing her rules. Up to the counter he saunters to pay with his Visa. "Your wife will find out when she gets the bill," she wants to call after him, but he turns back and winks. He knows.

Now she is outside a cafeteria, the entrance to a prison. It is like the cafeterias of childhood, with rich desserts spinning atop clear glass trays encased in a stainless-steel frame. Colorful layer cakes and fruit pies, puddings and Jell-Os, everything looks delicious. *But remember how nothing ever tastes as good as it looks?* About to walk through the cafeteria's glass door, she realizes that she has made a huge mistake. She can't go to prison. She is scared. The door is glass, and even if she does not die inside, she will be old by the time she comes out. Perish should be serving the time. Why doesn't he tell someone? Wanting to turn back, she is wrestling with how to undo what has already been decided when her eyes open, taking in sound and movement that ask her to consider, to make sense of, where she is.

"Lily?" It is unmistakably Joseph calling her, his voice speaking her name, which reaches down like a pebble dropped into swirling water.

Joseph?

"You're at the University Hospital," he says without prompting. "You're okay."

She is disoriented and scared; her head throbs, and every part of her body aches. She wants to ask him to hold her hand, but a large tube blocks her throat. Tears roll down her cheeks, and when Joseph bends over her to wipe them away, she can see that there are tears in his eyes, too. "You're going to be okay, Lily," he says again, brushing the damp hair away from her temples. "Just rest now."

She can see that her hands are strapped to her sides and attached to a maze of plastic lines, but she wiggles her fingers and stares down at them until he sees them moving and grasps them. His hand feels cool, her pain bleeding into his soft touch.

He sits with her while she closes her eyes, is still sitting with her when she opens them again. He is there to steady her quaking body, to witness her head jerking in a frantic motion he cannot understand.

The path is dark, lit only by moonlight reflecting off the wet tangle of vines that surround the house. She is grateful for the droplets of water that illumine her way, but they do not shine only for her. She enters through the splintery side door and hurries down the long hallway, pulling her children behind her, looking for the safest room. He is not looking for her children, but they must be protected, must not see what may happen, and because he is looking for her, she thinks he may not notice them under the bed.

"Hide here," she tells them, sees their faces smudged with dirt. "Don't come out until I tell you it's safe. Say nothing. Don't move."

But secret passageways are everywhere. Tunnels and holes. She must block every entrance. In her hands are two long nails and an old hammer. She must think carefully about the right place for the nails. Doorways are safe. She will use the two nails to fortify the closet door. But it is ridiculous to think that this will be enough. The hammer's head is loose; it does not drive the nails properly, and footsteps grow louder in the tunnel. Alone and exposed in the middle of the room, she knows there is nothing to do but wait.

Opening her eyes, alarmed, she can see Joseph watching her, eyebrows arched. His concern might possibly be suspicion, and her fear of the intruder quickly subsides to a stronger terror that her husband may know. Now she is glad for the tube down her throat; it will prevent any slips of the tongue. Let *Perish* gurgle deep down in her throat, rise with a hiss from her lungs. Her discomfort does not matter, is not the important thing. The tube will keep her safe, keep Joseph from knowing. Moving her head, she searches for Perish. He may be hiding in a corner where Joseph cannot see him. She is scared that he might be there. And she wants him to be there, watching her. But her eyes tell her that there are only machines surrounding her, sensors strapped to her chest and head and arms, two bleeping television screens emitting a continuous series of wavy green lines. She must be very careful here, in this place where every thought and bodily function is being monitored. And she wonders how her brain waves and the quickening of her heart might be read.

Wanting to ask where Jessie and Misha are, who's taking care of them, she furrows her brows, imploring him to answer the questions she cannot speak.

"Are you worried about the children?" he asks, reaching up to smooth her forehead. *Every thought is monitored and can be known.*

She nods.

"Jessie and Misha are at home. Loren is taking care of them. They're worried about you but not too worried. We told them you had to go to the hospital but that the doctors are taking good care of you and that you'll be home soon."

An image of her father perched on the side of his bed in his underwear takes shape, then disburses. Grimacing, she has no idea why she sees him that way.

"Don't worry," Joseph is saying, but even though he claims Jessie and Misha are safe with Loren, she can't help what she sees, and she worries.

"Can you remember anything?" he asks, perhaps forgetting that she cannot speak.

The old dead man returns, the one being cut open the day she stopped to see Joseph. It's the penis and purple nipples and perfect stillness that give him away, except that now his eyes are open and he is watching her. He is a bit frightening when she thinks about it, but she understands that he might view her as a comrade of sorts here in the hospital, which is not a friendly place. So that he will not misunderstand, she asks his forgiveness for staring at his sex and withered limbs. *They were remarkable!* she tells him, and she thinks she can detect a slight smile curling his atrophied lips. She knows it was a violation to gaze upon his body and do nothing when heart, liver, and bowels, the givers and takers of life, were lifted into the air and manipulated by strangers under the hot surgical lamps. But she thanks him for the raw knowledge of life and sex he has given her. She understands it now. *And it was displayed so exquisitely,* she says and laughs, hoping he will get the joke. *How could I turn away?*

Here in the hospital, detained under similar circumstances, she can see what each member of the team had been looking for that morning, and she wonders if they all will be satisfied with what they find. A secret held within the body that refuses to die. A confirmation of what was already suspected. She remembers the way Joseph yanked the limbs to break the rigor, his expert, cocksure handling of the organs, his intense concentration broken momentarily when he saw her through the glass. How he pulled down his gauze mask and raised a bloodied glove to his lips to blow her a kiss. He had waited a long time to do that. He had waited too long to show her such powerful expertise over the body. The way he exerted his might, sufficient to saw through ribs and to hold for her in his unshaking hands the body's secrets. She wishes he could know what she knows, here, with the dead man. Joseph will answer questions and make observations as the doctors and detectives do their work on her, but he hasn't a clue. He can never probe or coax from her the secrets contained inside her, secrets that she will not relinquish even in death. Perhaps this is all a rehearsal for what it's like in the end: strange and exposed for view and study and touch.

. . .

I t's crowded and very noisy. Nurses come with their carts to
draw blood, and she is wheeled down on a gurney for CT scans,
MRIs, EEGs, each test an attempt to locate trauma inside her
head until a green-suited respiratory therapist finally announces
that the tube can be removed from her throat. She is told to
exhale forcefully on the count of three, and when she does, the
tube is withdrawn, a bloody fish yanked up from her lungs that
makes her gag and gasp for air. Then Joseph is joined by neurolo-
gists and other specialists whose names clash glaringly with their
ugly, pedantic smiles.

The neurologist pulls rank and gets the first question. "Can
you tell us anything about what happened to you?"

"I'm sorry." She chokes, because even though the tube is gone,
she can still feel it scratching at her throat. "I don't remember
anything."

"That's okay." He is propitiatory, though whether about the
choking or memory loss she cannot be sure. "What is the last
thing you remember?"

"Losing my keys."

"Okay." Of course he has no idea what she is talking about,
but his voice assures her that this is all very normal. "And then
what happened?"

"It was hot. It felt like the hottest morning of the summer, and
the children were going to be late for day care."

She catches him rolling his eyes—a signal to Joseph?—as he
thanks her and leaves. The detectives arrive next, looking comical

and utterly serious. *Your color,* she wants to say, *it's not right.* But she can tell that these men are humorless; it is best not to joke with them.

The question, however phrased, is always the same: *Can you tell us anything about what happened?*

She wants to tell them how hard it is to know the desired answers and to want at the same time to placate everyone. She feels both powerful and bereft, knowing what each one wants, and still it is difficult to keep track.

E yes closed, she blames Perish for what is happening. She is angry with him because she needs him and he is nowhere to be found, and she cannot reach any conclusions without him. All this is not about her body, she tells herself, it is about coming to truth. She cannot survive here without Perish, cannot go on without him, and yet he has deserted her. Though she cannot remember exactly how it happened, his betrayal lurks in every corner of the room, in every face that bends over the bed to question her. What is true exists between them only in the darkness of motel rooms, in the friction created by their bodies. Without that she is lost, and she reaches a hand down between her legs, bringing a wet finger up to sniff not the smell of sex but the antiseptic rasp of chemicals, placed there without her knowing.

She wishes to die in the hospital bed with her secrets and lies. But under the white light, formless shapes move in and out, and voices human and not create sound from which she knows she cannot escape.

. . .

Her mother speaks constantly, but not in a language Lily might expect. When the doctors come, as they do each day to shine light in her eyes and probe her body, her mother reminds her: *Never let anyone know what you're thinking. Smile.*

It's a lie, Lily cries. *To smile when you're in pain. To purposely give the wrong information when they're just trying to be helpful.*

But her mother is relentless. *It's okay to lie; sometimes it's necessary. Truth creates a kind of space between people, and so do lies. Whether you tell the truth or make up lies depends only on what you want the space to look like.*

I married him because I loved him, her mother goes on. *There has never been anyone else for me.*

Lily stares blankly at the sealed windows and tight unyielding corners, listening to her mother. When her eyelids are shut and fluttering under the weight of dreams, she is listening. *Pay attention to how things look. Appearances reflect the state of the soul.*

And so what could it mean that her face spasms and jerks and wants to tell a story of its own, and what is she going to do about this story that she does not yet know and cannot hide?

All this cannot be good.

She strains to see Perish's face, but he is gone, eclipsed by others who do not matter, who position themselves awkwardly beside her with sorrowful faces that mock her. *What are you doing here? Go away*, she wants to tell them, but she doesn't. She heeds her mother's advice, smiles as she imagines pushing them from her sight, back onto the parched street where their faces will fry in the sun.

The department sends a cluster of potted primroses. They sit by the window, encased all day in their silent red shells, their faces opening only at night to greet the moon. She is grateful for them, for the way they grace the room with their simple beauty, and she thinks back to her first nights with Joseph, the cottage in Larchmont, the round moon that beamed into his room with its small rectangular windows. Now she has become the black moon, hidden by the earth with a story concealed behind her twitching face, and she no longer has the strength to fight against what she has become. Let the opening and closing of primroses narrate this space, so cut off from the world outside that it might be heaven or hell.

The question has been asked so many times that even against her will, it repeats in her head. *Tell me what happened.* Only she is not ready to know.

Not yet.

Her mother returns to chase away the fog. Comes to Lily as a house that she circles, noting how it rises magically into the sky from the back yet appears flat and low from the front. How can she resist entering such a house? Only once she is inside, it collapses into itself like a fallen cake, down and dark, and the air so cold and dense that it is hard even to move. She knows she should view from the outside what can be seen as beautiful, pristine, and very tall. But she stays inside, knowing she will never leave. She tells herself that she must stay because it is so invigorating to be inside. Or is it eviscerating? She knows, even as she asks which it is, that this question has no answer.

I married him, her mother says, the pitch of her voice strong and perfect, *because I didn't want to be lonely. There is no one else: no one.*

What can this possibly mean?

Joseph disappears from her bedside, but only after she pleads with him to go home, put the children down in the manner in which they are accustomed: they must have their teeth and hair brushed just so, must be offered sips of milk and stories (the fox and rabbit for Misha, which only she or Joseph can recite, and a different one each night for Jessie), must be kissed at least once on each cheek and told they are loved before the light is turned off. Even if their mother lies prone in a hospital bed, their bedtime rituals must go on smoothly, and must not be disturbed.

"How are they?" Lily is watching the primroses, their black stamens and pistils fully exposed against the night sky when Joseph returns, fatigue plainly visible on his face.

"They're fine," he says, distracted. "How are you?"

"Fine," she says. "But you don't look so well."

"I'm worried sick about you," he says, a bit sarcastically, she thinks.

"Why?" Even though she doesn't really want to know, the question slips from her mouth and cannot be retrieved.

"It's just pretty damn strange that no one seems to be able to explain anything," he says.

"The seizures?"

"No one seems to know what's causing them, but they've come up with some ideas."

His eyes dare her to ask what the ideas are, because up till now she has not asked anything. She would like not to ask, but her lack of curiosity is becoming suspicious, and she needs to hide it from him. "Okay," she says. "What's wrong with me?"

Joseph barely pauses to inhale before letting her in on a secret that he clearly does not wish to keep. "They're saying that the seizures are a result of trauma to your head, and that it's quite possible you were raped."

Raped. The word hangs in the air, refusing to fall. She tries to think of everything she knows about rape, to try on the word like a hat that does not fit but is worn conspicuously high on the brow. *One in four women will be raped in their lifetime, three out of those four by people they know.* "Why would they think I was raped?"

"You were found unconscious in a truck-stop parking lot. Someone called 911, but when the ambulance arrived, you were alone. In the middle of the day, in the middle of a truck-stop parking lot. Your students were waiting for you, Lily, but that's beside the fucking point. No one knew where you were."

Before it was the secret of her love affair that had threatened to destroy her. Now this secret knowledge is all she has to keep her safe. The morning. The children. The hot summer air. The feather lost along the highway, carried along by the wind only to be ground into the highway. Perish, the lovemaking between them ecstatic. Closing her eyes, she can feel herself falling into a kind of blackness that feels unholy and terrifying. She knows she was not raped. But she no longer trusts what she knows. "What makes them think I was raped?"

"You weren't wearing underwear. The paramedics found them under you, and when the doctors ran tests, they used a rape kit and found traces of semen."

"Yours?"

"They're only saying it's semen." Joseph shakes his head sadly. "It'll take at least a couple weeks before the tests are complete."

Raped. Lily's body shudders beneath her, and she can hear Joseph shouting for help. "*Seizure,*" he is saying, and a whir of motion begins outside her, in a place where she cannot be touched.

A local news crew gathers. She sees them on the television screen above her bed, watches a woman in a stiff red suit attempt to flag down her doctor as he enters the hospital. The same woman approaches Joseph, who meets her head-on, demanding with an outstretched hand that she go away. Joseph with his concentrated politeness and forceful demeanor. Lily is thankful for the space he provides, a human blockade protecting her from a world she cannot face.

In the end, the news story is brief: "A young female professor recently hired by the history department at the University of New

Mexico was discovered unconscious yesterday afternoon in the truck-stop parking lot outside the Four Winds Motel. Doctors suspect a head injury and have not ruled out the possibility of rape."

Memory floats like a feather drifting just beyond her grasp, and she reaches for it. Her children. A hot summer morning. Blood pools in her chest, causing pressure there that feels unbearable. Certain that her heart is failing, she rings the bell beside her bed. "I'm in terrible pain," she says, struggling up helplessly on her elbows. "I need drugs."

"I'll have to call your doctor," a conciliatory nurse tells her, then leaves.

She thinks she might want to stay like this, forever in convalescence, confined to a bed that arches and reclines with the push of a finger, in a place where her needs can be met by the ringing of a bell, drugs dripped into her arm on demand, meals carried in on trays. To be served and drug-ushered through her loneliness, incapable of doing harm to herself or others she loves. Exhausted and longing for an end, she cannot think what more there can possibly be.

"Considering what her body has been through," she hears the doctor reassure Joseph, "fatigue is to be expected."

Desire begets exhaustion begets hopelessness. Such a terrible state. She imagines she might die from it. Die for want of love, or even the memory of love that cannot be trusted. She wishes for something to hold, a treasured object tossed into the air—what difference does it make if no one is there to catch it when it falls?

D o you still love me?" she asks Joseph in the morning when he arrives to see her, then again before he leaves.

"Yes," he tells her. "Yes, and yes. Have you forgotten even that?"

H er mother appears as a fig. Heavy and white, she drops from the sky and lands soundlessly, a perfectly round indentation beneath the leafless tree. It's cold, even in the middle of summer. The snow falls and covers the fig, which should not be growing at this time of year. Perhaps the fig is really some kind of bulb that will shoot green leaves from the ground and blossom colorfully in the spring. Let the fig become a bulb, snow become dirt, summer become fall. No explanation can adequately describe this phenomenon. Yet it happens.

The confusing part is that she does not know which came first: the summer or the snow. The air-conditioning unit above her head pumps in cool air, masking the heat that she knows is outside but cannot feel.

W hose story should she believe? She, innocent, abducted from campus and raped, then dumped in a truck-stop parking lot. She, guilty and fully knowing, collapsed on her way to her car, having just spent the morning fucking her lover. The essence of both stories is similar: if she was kidnapped, then the reason she is here is completely beyond her control. If she spent the morning with Perish and collapsed in the lot, there is a kind of senselessness to the events that also feels right. Except for a void, one small detail that might never be reconciled. She wishes she had died. A sick irony, really, that she is still alive.

Her mother, a clear night in late fall, stars like an outstretched arm pointing the way home.

Dead. Perish. Gone.

The phone rings late into the night, and she answers it, groggy. "Are you alone?" the voice asks, and she recognizes it immediately.

"Just a minute," she says, casting her eyes around the room for Joseph. "Yes." Though he could be hidden behind a machine. She both wants her husband to be there and is glad he isn't. "At least I think I am."

"How are you?" he asks. There is a tremor to his voice that she identifies for certain as fear.

"Where are you?" she asks, refusing to answer.

"I'm in my office on campus."

"What time is it?"

"A quarter past midnight."

"What are you doing in your office?"

"Papers to grade."

"What does your wife think about all those papers?"

"Lily?"

"Yes. What?"

"I called to see about you, to find out how you are, not to talk about my wife. I'm not worried about her right now. I'm worried about you."

"Yes," she says. The answer is always yes.

There is silence, a sustained interval in which tears fill her eyes. She doesn't know why she is crying. Perhaps it is because the sound of his voice calling her back is as alluring as ever, and she already knows she will forgive him, has already forgiven him for what is unforgivable, and she hates herself for this inability to resist him. Perhaps she is crying because she is so happy to hear his voice.

"I've missed you," he says. "I've worried about you constantly."

"What happened?" she asks.

"What do you mean?"

"I need to know what happened, Perish."

"The morning we spent together?"

"Yes."

"You disappeared on me," he says. "I don't know. You went into the bathroom and turned on the shower, and when you came out, you said you needed to get to class. Then you dressed and walked out."

Pressing her palms hard against her eye sockets, she inverts her gaze to the lightning sprawls inside her head, the site where memory may lurk.

"I showered and then followed behind you, maybe five minutes later. I saw you across the parking lot as soon as I walked out
the door and ran back into the room and called 911. I didn't know
what else to do, Lily."

"You didn't even check to see if I was dead?"

"I knew you weren't dead."

"How could you know that?"

"Because I couldn't live without you."

Desire is the only thing that can make a wish real. She wants to
laugh at the way he has turned her own feelings against her.
And she wants to believe, too, that he knew, that he could
really know such a thing. Remembers the magical way he
appeared, grinning, behind doors that she opened, the way
their bodies responded to each other in some intuitive way that
might never be explained. She wants to believe in the desire
that binds them and will not let her die, but it seems more
likely that he couldn't have known, that all he really knew was
fear.

"What next?"

"I waited inside the room until the ambulance came. I swear,
Lily. I never took my eyes off you."

"You've heard the news story, then?"

"Which one?"

"The one that says I was raped. You know they have your
semen smeared on a slide downstairs in the lab. In their minds,
you will be a rapist."

"Never."

"Then tell me." She is begging now.

"You weren't raped."

"Tell me what happened, then."

"I don't know." He pauses.

"This is a ridiculous charade," she says between clenched teeth. "I should tell them the truth."

"You can't."

"Perish, an investigation is being conducted. They'll find out."

"They won't." There is silence. "I moved your car."

"You what?"

"It wasn't locked. I hot-wired it and drove it back to campus."

"Oh my God," she says. "You're a criminal."

"So you still desire me?"

"I desire you, and I think you're crazy."

"Look," he says. "If you don't tell them, they won't find out a thing. If you tell them, there will be a scandal. Everyone will be hurt. Neither of us should ever be caught in a situation like that."

"We are—" she is saying just as the nurse on night duty breezes in, shaking a thermometer. "Okay, I have to get my temperature taken now."

"I love you," he is saying as she hangs the receiver back in its cradle.

"Your husband?" the nurse asks, sliding a sterile sleeve over the thermometer and placing it under Lily's tongue.

She nods.

"Such a nice man." The nurse smiles into the machine,

watching as the electronic digits spin. "I once had a man like that."

Her temperature has returned to normal, but the nurse is no longer smiling. She is not a happy woman. Despair shows on her face, and it's scary to think of her as anything other than how she appears. Old, weathered, worried. Scary to glimpse a story Lily does not wish to see. *Perish is right,* she thinks. *A scandal would hurt everyone. He is right about most things.* A smart man. One of the reasons she fell in love with him. But he was wrong not to protect her from this. Wasn't that wrong?

There is a right way to do everything, and everything must be done precisely so. This will become obvious if you think about it. Dust before you vacuum, use a rag for dishes and a sponge for wiping surfaces, wash underwear separately from dishrags, don't eat anything for at least an hour after brushing your teeth.

Remember: I married him because I loved him. There has never been anyone else for me.

What is happening here, anyway? The bouts of dizziness and finally the seizure that left her unconscious. The body fighting the mind, vying for what is real. This is war, and even though what is at stake is not always clear, it will not end until one side wins. But what she understands now that she could not comprehend before is that for either side to lose means death for both. The mind cannot exist independently of the body; the body cannot exist independently of the mind.

Joseph drags her father in for a visit. Yas is a dog, forlorn and trailing behind as if tethered by an invisible lead. Ravaged from lack of care, he smells of piss and excrement, his body covered with a crusty layer of filth. "You need to help me out," Joseph says. Her father, she knows, is quickly becoming a symbol of what has gone wrong between them. A nagging hunch of Joseph's that the medical details only half explain what is wrong with his wife.

"He needs a shower," Lily tells him.

"You try." Joseph throws his hands into the air. "I've tried. Believe me, I've tried, but he'll have nothing to do with water or me."

"Maybe he can guess how you feel about him," she whispers.

Joseph's hands fall to his sides with a slap. "I am not the problem here," he says. "He's been whining all night, keeping the children up, acting like a disobedient brat. The problem, I'm afraid, is that he misses you."

"Really?" Lily looks hopefully from her husband to her father. "Do you miss me, Dad?"

Yas stands at the bed rails, engrossed for the moment in the control panel that moves the mattress up and down.

"Hmmm," Lily sighs, feeling herself being lifted then jerked back down.

"Look, I know you're probably not up for this." Lily can tell from the way Joseph stands with his shoulders and neck held rigid that he hasn't slept. "But I'm going to leave him here for a while. I've got to get to work for at least half the day; I'm way behind."

"Joseph, you can't!" Lily pleads with him. Dumbfounded, she presses the button on the IV monitor, releasing a dose of Dilaudid that she knows will relax her.

"What?"

"I'm in the hospital," she says weakly, feeling the drug surge through her veins. "They haven't let me get up in a week. I can't . . . I can't possibly watch him."

"I know," he says. "I know you're not in any shape to be doing this, but then neither am I."

She does her best to glare across the room at him, daring him with her eyes to relent. But he holds her stare, not even blinking, and in his stillness she reads all the mistrust and anger that has been building for months, maybe even longer.

"The nurses will never allow him to stay."

"Tell them he is your visitor," he enunciates through clenched teeth. "He *is* your father, for Christ's sake."

Her husband, beleaguered beyond capacity, is not making sense, but this battle, Lily knows, cannot be won. She can see the deep circles that ring his eyes, his ashen skin tone. He has remained at her side. Until now he has kept his ill feelings to himself, and she must give him something in return.

"Okay." Lily purses her lips. There is no choice about this one.

"He probably won't move anyway." Joseph lets his shoulders down slightly. It's hard not to feel sympathetic toward him. "He'll probably just sit there, and you can sleep, or whatever."

"Fine. No problem," she says, and her eyes fasten on Joseph's back as he walks away.

"Hi, Dad." She smiles sweetly. "Are you listening to any of this?" His face seems to have aged in her absence, his condition deteriorated. "Did Joseph tell you why I haven't been home with you? That I've been here in the hospital? Have you been worried about me?"

He stares blankly at her, recognition concealed tightly behind wrinkles and filth.

"I tell you what," she says after Joseph's back has passed from view. Turning and planting her feet on the ground, she rises slowly from the bed to test her balance. "You're going to spend the day with me, but you smell terrible. Really terrible. So you're going to get a shower."

"Come with me," she says, signaling for him to follow. "Hurry. Let's get you washed up without a scene."

The shower happens to be made for this type of work. She can stand at a distance and spray him with the nozzle without getting herself wet. Let him do the work, which, thankfully, he still knows how to do. She watches as he rubs the bar of soap between his hands, and she offers direction when he appears to lose his purpose. She watches carefully to make sure he doesn't forget to lather any part of his body, which she knows has not been cleaned for days. There was a time when such a task would have been too repulsive for her to imagine. A time when her body needed to be separate from his in an inexorable way. But that time has passed. Now the parts of him are as familiar to her as the baby's, and they evoke a kind of tenderness in her as she helps him out of the stall and dries him off with flimsy white hospital towels. She has not been on her feet in days, but the sight of him restores some kind of balance, and she does not falter in her movements.

"That was a lot of work, wasn't it," she says, feeling the need to lie down. He does not answer, but walks to her bed still wrapped in a towel and folds himself obediently between the sheets.

"That's my bed, you know," Lily says to him. But he seems not to care. What she knows is that her presence brings him peace, and she watches him after slumping in the chair beside her bed. She watches him watching her until his eyelids begin to droop and he settles in for a long sleep.

Jessie and Misha are not allowed to visit her on the fifth-floor unit. Hospital policy, too great a risk of contamination; hospitals are not safe places for children. But Joseph agrees to drive them by at the end of the day, and she sits looking out her window with nothing to do but wait, remembering how once, when she was a child, her father was hospitalized with gallstones. Back then, before laser surgery, the ordeal required days of hospitalization followed by recovery time on the couch. She remembers the clear plastic bag that hung from his side, collecting bile streaked with blood. Remembers the long scar that ran the length of his abdomen, how later it would remind her of a railroad track when she brushed a finger down it. But what she remembers most is the day her mother drove her to visit him, how he stood on a balcony wearing his favorite blue flannel bathrobe, waving down to her. How her mother stopped the car barely long enough to let her

wave—it was not long enough, too long—and how he tried to
appear stoic, his weight resting in a seemingly casual stance
against the IV pole that might have been a cane, the bulging bag
concealed beneath his robe. He waved to her and tried his best to
smile, to look like the father she remembered. She is sure of this.
But she knew.

Pressed up against the sealed pane, she can tell that the air
outside is hot. The sky is pale, thirsty after too much sun. People
move in slow motion, deadened by the afternoon heat. And she,
so close to that world though so removed, wonders if her children
will even recognize her from five flights down. And what will she
do when she sees them? Wave, of course. And smile.

She worries about what of that moment they might remember
when they are her age, what they will think of their mother.

I t's been too long. She has been away too long, and yet she is
surprised when the inevitable moment comes. "Good news,"
the doctor announces on morning rounds with a broad grin.
"We're letting you go home."

It is not clear why she has stayed so long, less clear why she
must leave, but she returns his smile. What choice does she have?
"Really?"

"No point in keeping you here, unless you can tell me something I don't already know."

"No."

Her bag is packed; Joseph is there to usher her home. The

children greet her with hugs and kisses, though she can tell that her absence has frightened them, diminished their trust in her. They are tentative, cautious, the way they act with strangers. "Did you miss me?" she asks.

"I missed you this much." Misha beams, spreading his arms as far as they will stretch.

"I missed you, too, Mommy," Jessie chimes, and the tears in her daughter's eyes make her weep. Her absence is unforgivable, she knows, a betrayal that might never be overcome. She knows she will be watched carefully from now on, every action scrutinized. But she vows to make up for her absence with hugs and patience and new stories before bed.

The monsoon season begins the day of her release, a dark layer of clouds that approach with a sudden flurry of wind and rim the Sandias. Clouds move across the sky, turning it black in minutes, leaving no patch of blue uncovered. Outside, under the portico with Loren and the children, she watches the storm approach. Great sweeps of wind catch trees off-balance and blow dust and gales through the humid afternoon air. Thunder echoes off the mountains while brave Jessie holds the wooden support beam, dangling her head into the storm to catch raindrops on her tongue. "Come and get me," she says, laughing, daring the rain to soak her. But when lightning strikes the nearby field, she rushes at Lily, jumping into her arms, almost knocking her over.

"It's okay." Lily draws her daughter's shivering body close, strokes her wet hair.

"Up, Mommy," Misha says from down below.

Rising from the bench, Loren walks over with arms held out. "I'll pick you up, Misha."

"No," Misha balks. "Mommy."

Lifting both her children high above the ground, Lily searches the sky for mountains made invisible by cloud cover; it is odd to see the familiar horizon completely hidden, no way without it to know for sure which way is up, and she wonders if the storm will ever pass. Her children are heavy, too heavy. It's been a long time since she carried them both this way, and she strains under their weight, trying out a song in Misha's ear as she paces under the portico.

"Shhhh." He quickly silences her. "Listen to the rain."

"Right," Lily concedes. He has never liked her singing.

Lily's arms feel like twigs, dangerously close to snapping. But Jessie's and Misha's arms encircle her neck, and her arms support their weight long enough to let the pain and the dramatic summer weather pass. Together they listen to the rain fall and watch the horizon until a patch of blue disperses the clouds, until as suddenly as it came, the storm is gone, leaving behind verdant, clear air that smells deceptively fresh.

L ily lingers outside as long as possible, not wanting to return to the house. *No turning back,* Perish once said, and yet she cannot stay away forever. She is happy that it is summer and that hot-weather dinners require little preparation. No stews or baked chicken. No pasta requiring water to boil on the stove. Lily offers the children Popsicles to eat outside while they wait for her to dream up a meal: chilled melon or gazpacho soup, cheeses, whole-grain breads from the local bakery, yogurt, fresh vegetables from their small garden. The cherries have turned from green to bright red, and she lets Jessie and Misha pick them, saving some for the birds. They wash and pit them and turn them whole into pie, which they eat warm with ice cream, leaving them sticky, sweet, and full. Popsicles before dinner, cherry pie for dessert, their despondent mother who performs all the motions necessary to keep them alive. Will they see her as faithful?

The heat does not let up; the swamp cooler running round the clock gives the air inside the house texture. She likes the way it smells, its scent as familiar as the sweat and play of her children, their love, and everything that has gone into the lives they have built and invented together. Lily paces the long hall that runs from her room past her children's, her father's, settling herself in her office at the end of the hall, finding comfort in the photos that line her desk—Jessie and Misha balanced on Joseph's knee, Jessie hugging Misha the night he arrived home from the hospital, dogs and cats and fish that they have adopted through the years. Her own writing fastened to the desk beneath rocks brought in from the yard by Jessie. The bookshelves she painted turquoise and topped with silly baubles important to no one but her because she remembers where each came from, and on the shelves, the children's books stacked alongside hers. All that is important appears in a tangle of color before her, looking exactly as it should.

"We know they were seizures," the doctor told her before she was released. "Status epilepticus. The tests we've run indicate what they were, but in the end we may never know what caused them. The thing to do now is to get on with your life. There is a chance, a very good one, that this might be the only episode, that nothing like this will ever happen again."

It is unprecedented. A fluke?

She does not call Perish, waits instead for the call she knows will come. And, of course, it does. "I want to fuck you," he says.

She is silent, not knowing how to respond.

"But I don't see how we can be together," he tells her.

"No," she agrees. "Things have changed, and I guess we've got to accept that."

"What's changed?"

"Everything and nothing."

"While you were in the hospital"—he pauses, and she hears in his voice the tenor of fear, as familiar to her as heat rising off his body—"I made love to my wife."

"Okay." Having paced the hall, she settles in the bathroom. Hunching over the countertop, the phone pressed between her ear and shoulder blade, she lets the cool tiles numb her fingertips while she assesses her face in the mirror. The news has changed nothing. Her lips, her eyes, *she* is the same. Reflected back at her is the face he has undoubtedly memorized, the face she thought he loved. "Why?"

"I had to. Don't you understand?"

"No," she says. "I don't. Not at all."

"I still love you, Lily, still desire you. I will always be in love with you."

"I have to go," she tells him.

"No," he says. "Please don't go."

Her head feels empty, but an intense pain burns under her skin, and she knows that deceit is far less subtle than the truth. Oddly, she believes everything he has ever told her. Believes that he loves her, and that his betrayal does not diminish it. But she is learning something about marriage, too. Even though Perish has told her stories of his wife, the one he claims not to love, he's been married to her for almost as many years as Lily has been alive. They have a history that she will never be part of.

"Lily, I did what was necessary. That's all I can say. From the first time I met you, I have wanted only you. I can never be in love the way I am with you, but I know I can't have you, and I have to find some way to go on with my life."

She who sleeps nightly encircled in her husband's arms, what can she say? But it is not the same. They are not the same. This is not the way it's supposed to go, she is certain of that. He is the senior professor; why has this not occurred to her until now? His reputation is established, his credentials beyond question. She is the fledgling scholar, her efforts evidenced by a single book. It is enough to have gotten her the job, but that will not be enough to sustain her. She carefully constructs a story: sexual harassment. He understands her, and he has *deceived* her. She will make it her work to bring him down. But the story quickly vanishes. She is tired. Her eyelids are puffy from crying. She sees him as clearly as she sees herself: imprisoned in a life that is a farce, the goodness that was her marriage made impossible by her desire of Perish.

It's over, she wants to tell him. There is no turning back from the truth; she knows that. But the words stick in her throat, and she says nothing.

She is thankful that there is always something to do. Running through the motions of her day, stopping first at the day-care center to drop off her children, then driving through a series of errands. There is always something more that can be done. A mother's story. A wife's story.

Key in the ignition, groceries in the trunk, she hears the crunch of metal behind her and turns to the busy street, where a yellow school bus has collided with a small white pickup truck. Rows of children flash before her, the long hair of young girls snapping into quick S's as their bodies lurch forward then crash back against the hard-rimmed seats. She imagines them reclining, unconscious, their necks exposed. Leaving her car to run for the bus, she holds an image of Jessie in her mind, her five-year-old who is still so vulnerable and must be saved.

But as she climbs into the bus, she can see it is empty. The bus driver stands on the curb, talking quietly to the driver of the pickup, who rubs his head as he studies the bed of his truck, bowed like the back of an angry cat. There are no children aboard the bus. Either they have disappeared or, more likely, they were never there.

. . .

Perhaps, she thinks, if the mind plays tricks on itself long enough, it begins to erode, like sand washing away from the shore. *It's a beautiful thing,* she tells herself. Steep cliffs that angle down to the water; lines visible even in the desert along the red buttes and ridges that lead to canyon streams.

"That's how the earth was formed," she told Jessie when they visited Oak Creek Canyon and her daughter wanted to know how the mountains got their shape and color. "Over many, many years, the water has receded from the land. It's the natural progression of things. It's something you can count on." Like her mother tucking her into bed every night of her childhood, reassuring her through hugs and kisses that the world would not end when Lily closed her eyes for sleep, the same gestures she offers her children every night. She tries to think but can't remember how or when that ritual ended.

It's summer, and the house no longer belongs only to them. With the rain beating steadily on the roof, Joseph wakes Lily, dragging her out of bed to help him catch a mouse he has seen scurrying beneath the kitchen table and into the linen cabinet. While he stands behind her, waving a flashlight vigilantly from above, she, bleary-eyed, empties one drawer at a time, surprised to find children's toys stuffed between cloth napkins and tablecloths, scraps of paper with telephone numbers and notes that no longer make sense, a half-eaten carrot. "This is incredible," Lily cries. "This is horrendous." How have they managed to accumulate so much junk? And how could they not have known about the mice when their droppings are everywhere?

"Shhhh." Joseph puts a finger over his lips, admonishing her, making her believe that silence is part of trickery. Armed with a plastic bowl and a newspaper, his job is to spot the unsuspecting prey and quickly scoop it up.

But the mice maneuver in and out of impossibly small cracks and holes, stealing crumbs from the counters, leaving black feces like Hansel and Gretel's bread crumbs, trails leading to nowhere. There is also the hantavirus, which is no small fear. Traps must be set, which means the children must be warned so as not to get fingers snapped off, and dead mice in the morning to dispose of before coffee. No one wants to be the first one up.

Joseph suspects that the seasonal rains have brought the rodents indoors, but Lily thinks of them as a curse. She tracks their droppings around the house, looking without success for their point of entry. Then there are the insects. Earth babies appear in the children's room, their huge, oval bodies so anemic they might glow in the dark, or mistakenly be picked up like something that rolled out of a gumball machine for a quarter. There is the centipede that slithers up the bathtub drain, the Arizona stinger with its ugly pincers and sharp, mean body that even the dogs won't touch. Brown and black spiders cast webs from the beams overhead, as if daring Lily to open her eyes from bed and read messages in the intricacy of their new designs. But mostly, these days, there are crickets. They leap through the house, teasing the dogs, clacking and chirping when everyone should be asleep. Occasionally a dog will pounce, but what then? Their intent is never to kill, only to play or to maim, so these are mutant one-legged and half-eaten crickets. Joseph tells the children that crickets are good luck, and so it is a bad thing to kill them. He shows Lily how to trap them beneath plastic cereal bowls, sliding a magazine beneath carefully so as not to amputate crooked legs and spindly antennae, scooping them up and flinging them into the bushes outside to eat other bugs.

"Are you still in love with Daddy?" Jessie wants to know before bed, her arms and legs entwined around Lily's waist.

"What do you think?" It is likely another of Jessie's many stalling techniques, to stay up a moment longer and inspire her mother to yield one more story before sleep. Lily is aware of this, but curious also as to how her feelings for Joseph are being read by her daughter, remembering how Jessie once shocked her by observing, "Daddy loves you, but you don't love him."

"Why do you say that?" she'd asked.

"Because it's true."

"I think you're in love," Jessie says enigmatically now, letting Lily drop her into bed.

"Hmmm." Lily smiles down at her daughter. "So what makes you ask such a question?"

"Well, I understand how people fall in love, but Miranda's parents don't live together."

"That's because they're divorced."

"But when you get married, you promise to stay together forever, right?"

"Yes."

"So once people get married, why don't they stay in love?"

"Jessie." Lily pecks her daughter's eyelid then rubs the tip of
her nose over her cheek to make her giggle. "You have very interesting ideas about things, and that makes you very wise, but
sometimes I have no answers for you."

"I am very smart," Jessie concedes with a sigh.

"It's not good to think too much," Lily cautions before turning
out the light.

Lily returns outside to drink wine with Loren under the portico, their usual spot, while they watch the last traces of light
disappear from the evening sky. "Such a pretty night," Loren says,
emptying her glass and reaching for the bottle.

"Yes." Lily lets Loren fill her glass. Without trees to obscure
the view, she can see for miles in all directions. She wonders
whether the clouds over the Sandias to the east and the Jemez to
the west will retreat or come together, bringing more rain.

"I like spending time with your children." Loren kicks off her
shoes and plants her feet on the bench, hugging her knees to her
chest. "If I ever have children, I hope they'll be as good as yours."

"Thanks." Lily smiles. "Thank you for taking care of them; I
owe you for that."

"No problem. Maybe I *will* have children, just so you can
return the favor."

"If you're lucky, Jessie will be old enough to baby-sit."

Looking over at her friend, Lily wishes she could issue some kind of warning: *Don't get married; don't have children.* No one ever offered her such advice, and she knows she wouldn't have followed it even if they had. For as far back as she can remember, she always knew she would have children, knew, too, that she'd get married because she didn't want to raise them alone. But nothing has prepared her for what life looks like now: her body the glow of a seamless existence, everything she'd always dreamed about held inside her like a promise, like the flowers in her father's garden bursting into bloom with a show of color that took her breath away. So why can't she appreciate the life she's worked so hard to create, and why doesn't there seem to be anything to live for? She's begun to doubt nightly that she'll wake up in the morning. To steal the thought and carry it secretly in dreams and let it appease the misery she can't explain, except that she fears her life is slipping away from her.

What's wrong, Lily? The question is being voiced, but she does not know the answer. Perhaps it has to do with how she never felt she had a choice about anything. How everything she did was in some way determined by her mother, by anticipating her wishes and working with them, or by working against them, as she did when she knew that Lily's remaining at home was no longer possible. All this was, in some way, inevitable. But perhaps this is merely the consequence, equally inevitable, a moment when she knows she must choose a path even though nothing at all is clear. Her job at the university, her husband, her father, her children, her lover. They inhabit her, each filling her as urgently as her own desires, but each separate and distinct, and she can no longer contain the whole. The fullness has turned to emptiness, and a despair unlike anything she's felt blinds her.

"Lily, what's wrong?" Loren calls to her.

"What?" She blinks up at the planets now dotting the sky. "What do you mean?"

"Have you heard anything I've been saying?"

"I'm sorry, Loren," she says, feeling the air has been sucked from her lungs; the seizures were merely a warning, a symptom of a life coming undone. "I don't know what's wrong."

"Are you having seizures again?"

"No. It's not that."

"Is it the rape?" Loren's question shocks her. In the silence between them, the deep, throaty hum of bullfrogs reverberates in her chest, and she realizes that the noise has been there all along, undetectable until now. Perhaps sensing that the children have gone to bed, a line of quail stroll across the stucco wall, and five rabbits appear to feed on the lawn, unperturbed by the dogs lying around her feet, disinterested in something so familiar. It's peaceful here, just outside of the city, where lights from across the river flicker as noiselessly as fireflies. Low in the sky, the last swallows dart and swoop along with a stray bat, picking bugs out of the darkening sky.

"I wasn't raped," Lily confides.

"So you've remembered what happened?"

"No, I don't remember anything, but I know I wasn't raped."

"You know, I've been raped."

"Oh, God." Grabbing at her glass of wine, Lily takes a huge

swallow. She has a sudden urge to confess everything, tell her that she is not the person Loren thinks she is, not at all. She has lied about everything, and she doesn't deserve or even want this pity. Longs instead for some sort of honesty that will let Loren decide whether she should be her friend.

"You don't have to tell me, Loren," she says. "I want to hear whatever you want to tell me, but you should know that what's happened to me is different from whatever happened to you."

"I know," Loren says, falling silent. "My father was a drunk, and he used to come into my room at night when he thought I was sleeping. I went through years of therapy as an adult because of it. It took years to even be able to admit that to myself. But it's not anything I talk about, except to say that it happened."

"I'm sorry," Lily almost whispers. Loren's silhouette shines ghostly in the falling darkness, her fair skin and pale blue eyes catching whatever light remains in the sky. She looks mysteriously beautiful and very fragile, and Lily knows that her own secrets are no greater than anyone else's, and she wonders how people find a way to live with their pain.

"Life is like that, I think. Things happen, and when they're really terrible, you tell yourself they're not happening or that they weren't so bad. You know, I kept thinking when you were in the hospital how happy you were when I met you. Didn't you say last summer that you thought you had the perfect life? I liked you because of that, because I'd never known anyone who could say that, but it seemed somehow genuine coming from you."

"I remember." Lily smiles. "It was genuine."

"You still have the perfect life," Loren reassures her. "A husband who loves you, two beautiful children, a great job. Good friends——." She laughs.

"Loren, stop." Lily takes a deep breath and exhales the words. "I had an affair."

"I know." Loren wrinkles her brow, then lets her body relax. "I mean, I think I knew. I think some part of me knew."

"I haven't told anyone," Lily says.

"It happens." Loren shrugs. "It happens all the time."

"I came so close to losing everything," Lily says, not hearing Loren, choking on her words. She can feel her dinner rising in her throat, and she wonders if that's the way the truth feels when it comes out, or perhaps it's the deceit of the last months leaving her. "I probably shouldn't have told you, but I didn't want you to feel sorry for me. It's not like you think." And she begins to laugh. "It's worse."

Loren laughs, too, but in a circumspect way that ends like an interrupted sentence. "Is it over?"

"Yes." Lily sighs. "It didn't mean anything, but it just about ruined my life." She hates how trite this sounds. She'd wanted to reveal something true about her life to Loren—to feel close to her. But how, she wonders, can intimacy ever be forged when she has managed not to say what she means about anything? What she wants, she realizes, is to restore the kind of intensity that seems to have vanished from her life. But Loren is a stranger; she's a neighbor, not a friend, and Lily guesses it would be wrong to pretend otherwise.

"You will get through this, you know." Loren grasps her hand from across the table. A gesture, Lily hopes, of forgiveness, and she wills herself not to recoil from the touch.

"I will, you're right." Lily smiles. She knows Loren wants her to say more, to add the information necessary to substantiate her confession, convince Loren how hard she's tried to hold everything together. But who knows where Loren's sympathy lies, and what does she know about Lily, anyway, besides what she's learned from watching the children. Wishing she could take back what she's said, Lily pulls her hand back from the tabletop and slaps her wrist as if to swat a mosquito.

"You know, if you don't love Joseph, you should leave."

Lily dismisses the anger she suddenly feels. She wonders what Loren could possibly be seeing, but she is afraid to ask. "I love my husband," she says.

So what should the shape of the space between Joseph and her look like? Should it be round like the moon, or a perfect rectangle framing the night sky? Later, watching Joseph eye her as she undresses for bed, she feels a sudden twang of shyness and reaches into her dresser for a nightgown. The air is warm and humid after the storm. She doesn't need a nightgown, doesn't think she even owns one, but digging beneath piles of underwear, she dredges up one that he bought her one year as an anniversary gift.

"Remember this?" She laughs, smoothing the wrinkled silk.

"I do now." He smiles. "Vaguely."

It's white and as soft as skin. She slides it over her head, trying to hide her body from him, yet knowing the ridiculousness of such an effort. He knows the shape and feel of her intimately, knows how her skin stretched and ached through one pregnancy and then another, knows where she is most tender, where most aroused. He is the man who stood watching while blood surged from her womb; watched under the white birthing lamp the dark heads of their children, matted with blood, crowning inside her like dahlias; watched as the doctor pressed against her bloated abdomen to coax out the afterbirth, huge and ugly as it slid from her. He is the man who has held her shivering through the fever of flu and tears, kissed the first breath of morning from her lips, and sworn with a wry smile that she has always smelled of roses. He has endeavored to create lies to please her, and accepted hers without flinching, never wishing for a perfect life but holding out every night for a good one. Knowing that he still desires her, she thinks that love is as mysterious as it is problematic.

After sex, Lily asks, "What does it feel like—I mean, what do I feel like to you after all this time?"

"Has it been that long?" A smile tugs at his lips, but his eyelids are heavy, and she knows that he's nearly asleep. "We're getting old," he says absently.

Lily, who often feels herself growing old, has never thought the same about Joseph. To her, he is forever youthful, somehow in her mind younger than she.

"I have five gray hairs in my beard," Joseph says, tilting his chin up so that she can count them.

"I'm serious," she says, dejected.

"It's been a long time," he concedes. "But not really, considering I once promised to love you for the rest of my life. There's a way to go before we're old together, don't you think?"

"What matters to you, then? I don't really know what to believe anymore."

"You matter to me," he says, reaching a hand across the bed

and stroking her belly. "I remember looking at you and knowing for the first time in my life that I could love someone forever."

"But what is it like?" she insists.

"Why do you do this to me," he says, "when I'm so tired?"

But she will not let it go, not yet. Turning over, she straddles his chest, letting her hair veil his face.

"Being in love with you is like being with anyone." He says these words not in passion but in a dreamy half-sleep that appears to have overtaken him, and she slides off to her side of the bed, letting him drift into sleep alone.

What could he possibly mean? She knows he's always desired her, promised to love only her, but she imagines it is his commitment to her that allows him to speak these words. To him, she is anyone. She brushes a finger down the steep ridge of his nose, wanting to plant herself in his sleeping brain.

It is dizzying to grasp in infinite darkness for something that no longer exists, to hang on to the mere memory of a life that once stretched and contracted as surely as a beating heart. Faint reverberations still heard like sound muted by waves; waterlines visible along the incline of ancient cliffs mark the past, palpable indicators of erosion and all that is inevitable.

Go there, she must. With an open heart, open hands. Wanting to receive. The mother with barren breasts, flesh torn away by hungry insects, dissipated by time. What is perfect can exist only

in memory. Perfection, she knows—perhaps has always known—
does not suit reality, unless it is in the form of Jessie and Misha,
still so innocent. And memory is not enough.

L ily." Perish's voice lingers like a ghost in the phone line. "It
was over long before it was gone. I understand that now. I
want to be with you."

"I don't know." She stalls because she can feel her pores opening, her body letting in air through the skin. It is not supposed to
work this way. She holds her breath, but air enters her body anyway, and she clenches her jaw to keep her teeth from chattering.

"Wait," he says. "I may know something. I've been thinking
more about your father. He had a sad start in the world. I'm not
saying you need to feel sorry for him, but I *am* a historian. I know.
He came upon his flaw honestly.

"When your mother died, the joy went out of his life. Then
you wouldn't talk to him anymore, but you were all he had. The
fucking plants meant nothing to him after that. They all died
within a year, and not because he forgot to water them. He
couldn't grow anything alone. And without the plants, there was
nothing to do. He started to forget things. He really did lose it.
You thought you owed him your life, because you remembered
who he had been. When you were growing up. When your mother
was alive. But you don't owe him anything. Think about it."

"What are you saying?"

"I know of this great store in New York that specializes in

exotic birds. I want to take you there. I'd been thinking I wanted
to buy you a finch, but now I know it's got to be a phoenix. We'll
set it in the window over the park, and it can sing all day while we
make love. Or we can throw a sheet over its cage and you can sing
to me."

"I can't sing."

"Then I'll sing to you."

"I've never heard you sing."

"I have perfect pitch. Trust me."

D ad." She takes a minute to sit with him before leaving. "I
have to go out. Will you be all right here? Can you take care
of yourself?"

He smiles, a look she chooses to call lucidity. It is a smile from
her childhood, long since forgotten. Guileless, anxious to please.
She could swear, though she realizes it can't be true, that he
knows, and she doesn't want to leave him because of it.

"You don't need to tell Joseph anything, but can you give the
children hugs for me? Tell them I love them. Tell them I will
always love them."

She wants to believe that somehow he understands a thing she
doesn't, a thing he can't know, and she wraps her arms around his
shoulders, surprised when she shouldn't be that he doesn't
respond.

"No getting into trouble, okay?"

He is still smiling when she backs out of his room, pulling the door shut with a click. Standing in the hall, listening for a signal that isn't coming, she knows Joseph will be home soon with the children. She doesn't want to go, but she must hurry, and after bolting the front door behind her, she rushes to her car.

It must be over a hundred degrees in the sun. Sweat begins pouring down her back the instant she touches the seat, and she tells herself as she drives away that the moisture pooling along her spine is not fear.

Four

Lily at thirty-five. Can a flower in full bloom know its short life? See the sweat glistening like dew in the summer sun? Her fingers wrap around the steering wheel; they are soft and white and pliant as petals, but deceptively strong. Air creates a steady current against the car, and clouds hover. It is dizzying to traverse this familiar route, traveled countless times with the children, made different today.

Albuquerque is an ugly city, really. The low mesas to the west sink each day under the weight of ready-made structures, and along the highway new restaurants, hotels, and office complexes shroud the land, forcing prairie dogs and coyotes to uproot or die. All that is not of the earth steals from the city its only distinction. The Sandias are the only constant, rising not far to the east as if to assure Lily she will never be lost. She accepted their presence the day Joseph signed his contract with Health Sciences and she signed hers with History, the same day they put a mortgage on the house. But they have always had a haunted, desolate look to them. Only the sky is beautiful, the clouds rising with perfect balance over the crest of the mountain range, amassing like a warning in the clear blue sky.

Lily keeps her eye on the path the clouds take as she drives, thinking how there is for each person a particular landscape that feels right, and how New Mexico is the place Joseph has always called home. She has appreciated through his eyes the harsh beauty of the desert, its subtle colors and truth. It is like Joseph's face, his bleached skin and freckles, the soft wrinkles and gray hairs he makes her examine that have recently begun to mix with the blond ones in his beard. It is something you can't see unless you are looking, and she has been trained to see. Old age will suit him. He will be steady as a stone and wise, revealing prominent bones through a loosening and thinning of skin. She doesn't know why she finds herself thinking about her husband, projecting him through time as she is leaving him. It's odd how a face she hasn't tried to imagine in months seems clearer as she drives away.

At the airport, the ticket agent announces the fare to New York. The price is so ridiculously high that Lily expects an apology. She waits, and when it does not come, she hands over her credit card, pretending not to hear. The transaction is conducted in a blinding silence, then she answers questions, resolutely signs her name, and walks away waving a boarding pass. She is rooted in her clunky heels yet tall, gliding as she moves as if pulled upward by an invisible stem. But what is she doing at the airport without even a suitcase? Her children—she looks down at her watch—will probably already be home, along with her husband, wondering where their mother could have disappeared to this time. But she cannot think about them, does not even know how to begin when she sees Perish already sitting at the gate. She sees his foot before she sees the rest of him. Dangling restlessly in midair, it does not stop moving. One leg horizontal, the real one a V over the one that isn't, the foot bobbing like a sinker tugged by the play of a fish on the line.

"Hey," she says, still not daring to meet his gaze. "Catch anything good?"

He smiles, either not understanding or not hearing, rises to hug her before lifting a small travel bag from the seat beside him so that she can sit, so that they can wait like two strangers expecting different sets of arrivals. This should be a joyous occasion, she tells herself, this moment they have waited to make happen. But maybe the moment has already passed. They sit quietly, watching departures that might be dramatizations of their own.

The plane ascends to the east, lifting off on time against the setting sun with a pressure that pushes Lily against the seat and causes the muscles in her face and neck to stiffen. Perish shifts uncomfortably and does not relax until the flight attendant appears at his side. He orders a gin and tonic, a double, which he sips greedily. Lily does not look at him until he speaks to her, his speech slowed by alcohol in a way that invites a response. He holds his head carefully upright and smiles at her with half-shut eyes, a picture of her forming with each blink and swallow of gin.

"So do you suppose we've crossed the state line?" he asks, not really curious, she thinks, but wanting to hear his own voice.

"No." She gazes out her window at the spottiness of piñon that stretches over the darkening desert. "New York is still a long way off," and then she closes her eyes, settling in for the distance.

J essie is the land, her skin the color of dawn as it spreads like wings pulsing through the morning sky; Misha is the trees, his hair the dark paste of an old elm. He is what grows out of the earth, spreading roots below and reaching into the sky with a confidence that might seem naive outside of nature. Jessie is light to Misha's dark, she is the vastness of land and air and imagination, and Misha is all body. Perhaps it is the difference between Lily and Joseph, female and male, pronounced in their children. Why else could it be that Jessie can enter so freely into the liquid world of feeling, plunging beneath the water's surface, while Misha must scrutinize everything in pendulous swings between pleasure and anger.

Lily remembers Jessie's attempt to explain to Misha one night before bed about the transcendent. "Everything beautiful is made by God," she told him with a kiss good night. "God is in the air and in the trees—invisible and everywhere."

"Where?" Misha asked, his eyes wide open in the darkness. "I can't see anything."

"I just told you," Jessie insisted. "God is everywhere."

"Is God here with us?"

"Yes. Everywhere."

"I don't think so," he announced defiantly. Lily watched as he paused to think, then stared at his sister blank-faced.

"It doesn't matter what you think." With this Jessie dismissed him, turning away from him to face the wall.

Credulity, a tendency to believe. Why is it, Lily wonders, that Jessie possesses what Misha lacks, and that Misha's inherent cynicism complements so perfectly his sister's faith? They need each other, she decides. They are land and ocean, forgiveness and strife, gone here in the sky where air blows in from overhead vents like stale breath exhaled by some mechanical god. The stars outside are so close she imagines she could grab a fistful and carry them home to her children in a basket of shimmering light.

Back on the ground, the sun has already set, but up above, the sky is rich with color and waves of light. She likes the feeling of being somehow above her life. It is, she considers, not unlike the world of dreams, where everything matters but has no literal value.

"What are you thinking?" she asks Perish. His arm encircles her, but his gaze has shifted from her to the box window.

"I'm thinking how I should feel light instead of leaden, like my weight alone could make this plane come down."

She doesn't know which scares her more: the thought of the plane crashing to the ground or the weight of Perish pressed up against her. "Try thinking light thoughts," she proposes.

"Any suggestions?"

"Think about picking me up and spinning me in slow circles." The ritual she and Perish performed in motels, like Jessie's on a smaller scale when she was still an infant, wagging her head at the sight of Lily's breast—a primitive instinct that always ensured she would be filled with milk the instant her tiny mouth latched on to the nipple. It's the spiral of history, Lily muses, this moment she is trying to create in his mind, a replication of their mating ritual and of Jessie's nursing habits as an infant, all points along a line running to the spiral's center.

"Can't do it." He brushes a finger across her cheek. "I'll throw up."

He does look nauseated, she thinks. Or is it her own face she is remembering, their meeting over pizza the night she realized how much she had already lost when she agreed to see him for dinner. She decides to attribute Perish's pallor to the plane's bumps and dips and prays they don't run into turbulence.

"Now what are you thinking?" she asks.

"I'm wondering what they'll do in History when neither of us shows up for classes tomorrow."

"They'll probably have a good laugh." Lily clears her throat nervously, knowing how hard she's tried to be careful. This final decision was inevitable; wasn't it?

"I don't care what they do. I wouldn't be here if I cared."

"Guess what *I'm* thinking."

"Let's see," he says, gazing through the shadows that line her face in the dark. "You're thinking that you should have brought a toothbrush."

"No." She laughs. "But I should have."

"I might let you use mine."

"Thank you. I might accept."

"Do you always travel this light?"

"Usually," she sighs, "I have a diaper pack over my shoulder, along with a cooler for snacks, a change of clothes, toys, you name it."

"Then this is a pleasant exception." He grins. "I always pack the same thing. Two pairs of jeans, two rolled-up shirts, under-wear, socks, and a toothbrush."

"I thought about what I'd take with me." She speaks softly, as if to herself. "I had a suitcase out and everything, but in the end I couldn't fill it."

L ying in the dark, a child on either side, she once created imag-inary boxes. "They are rather ordinary-looking," she told them. "Just four sides of cardboard." Light enough to be carried through the house in thin arms. "But they're magic, because you can fill them with a wish, one for each of you, and you can wish for anything. Anything at all," she explained, "and it will come true."

Jessie asked for a television set on which she could project any image she could imagine and make it real. Good. Lily waved her arms to produce from the air a television, which she dropped lightly into the box.

Misha wanted a star pulled down from the sky. A star to string on a chain and wear around his neck so that he could admire it when it was not being kept for him in the box. They were too young to know that for Lily, a wish conjured up not what was hoped for but what was lost.

"If you could have anything, what would you wish for?" she asks Perish.

"I'd wish for a different life," he says. "One where leaving and staying meant the same thing."

She smiles, seeing the worry lines etched on his face. Her hand glides to her own face and feels for the beginning of wrinkles. It's odd, how old she can feel next to him, yet how young, and how others' perceptions of her have always set the pace of her life, once accelerated, now thrown back to a time she knows should have passed long ago. She wants to steer him off the subject of wishes, to remind him that he is part of a trip from which she does not plan to return.

The walls of the plane are thin, the interior hollow, like marriage, which is itself a sort of tunnel. Dark, insular, safe. Joseph at her side at all times, calling to her to journey as if she were blind, except that there is a difference between being blind and traveling with your eyes closed.

Now the walls of the tunnel encircle her. They are curved, creating the illusion of space where there are only walls. Perish. She calls to him. Her heart flutters when she feels in her center the place occupied by him. He is here with her, the impossibility of a love that holds her and will not let her go. You slide your hands up and down, gaze ahead for an opening that is still so far off. When, and how might she emerge? Perish's arm presses against hers; the space between them is narrow, and the dimmed lights make it hard to see. She turns her head slightly, as if suffering from stiffness in the neck, and it occurs to her how severely restricted her movements are. She has been leaving for a long time; a long, tiring journey has led her to this flight, to sit next to Perish, to share this fragmented moment. She wonders how it can be that a lifetime dissembles and reassembles simultaneously, loss and recuperation passing with a familiar glance as they follow their trajectories.

L et him come to her with his past; let her become a screen upon which images can be projected. View the shapeliness of a simple geometric life. A house overlooking trees, as if its foundation were built of air. As if it might be possible to step out on the balcony and keep walking.

"The bird," Lily muses. "Were you serious about the bird?"

"Of course I was."

"Well, I've been wondering," she says. "What will it eat?"

"Bird seed," he says, unperturbed.

"Okay," she says. "But I've never liked the idea of keeping a bird in a cage. It seems unfair."

"Then we'll let it fly around."

"Won't that be messy?"

"What do you mean?"

"Bird shit."

He laughs, pressing her head against his shoulder. "You think too much. Get some sleep."

She does, and it's a hungry kind of sleep, chaotic and restless in its movement across land and over water. She has lost something that she must find. Her life depends on it, but she keeps getting caught in tall trees and barricaded by miles of ocean, seemingly impossible to cross.

. . .

She dreams she is inside the ocean, taking saltwater into her lungs and pumping it out like breath. She is surprised to not be drowning, and when she steps off the plane well past midnight, the air settles like wax in her lungs. The dank, familiar dirtiness of New York blows in off the water, proudly announcing her arrival in a place that does not care she has returned. How could she ever have left? How can she not love such a city, coax it back into memory? There are too many things that cannot be known, and love is ultimately mysterious. How two people find each other and what to do then. Seeds planted or scattered by the wind or dropped from the beaks of birds.

It is dizzying to be back in the city, but she reads the signs well, remembers Perish once telling her that he could read signals only in the woods. *He doesn't belong anywhere east of the Mississippi,* she remembers thinking. And she was right. He seems lost here, so far from the earth. But she is home in this place where randomness and gaps of logic combine to make perfect sense.

The city is the light of the mind, a landscape where every building must be measured before taking its place between earth and sky; where the park of imported and carefully selected trees is mapped on a grid to hold the center, and carriages circle concrete paths within, leaving in their wake the faint, clipped echo of horse hooves; where zoo animals sleep behind bars, and news is made when a coyote creeps down from Westchester through the Bronx to hunt in the open field. Steel skyscrapers and bridges, cafés and subways collect and diffuse their enormous energy. Once constructed by people, they now assume an ungodly life of their own, surviving each day oblivious of the hands that created them.

L̲ily, delicate and beautiful flower of death: how is it that she has left her mother? Betrayed her husband? Led Perish away from his life without flinching? She had thought that she might die, but is it callous that she will not repent? Does a flower know its short life?

She steers Perish left on Thirty-eighth Street, toward the hotel. Stale air hangs in the chamber created by tall buildings, and she shivers despite the humid warmth that clings to her body. She is alone with Perish, and it is night. She has journeyed to hotels with Perish many times before, but never at night. They stop along the edge of the East River to kiss, and she shifts her gaze from the light bouncing off the water to the cluttered night sky, and she feels the space between water and sky opening like a womb to which she has returned. Her entire life, or what is left of it, spans the horizon. So why does she not feel elated? Why is it that liberation must always be coupled with fear? Why has she not known this until now? Perish might think he knows her, but he doesn't. He may as well be a stranger stopping beside her to take in the view. He smiles, but not at her. She exists inside a possibility, and her mother comes to her in the gap. A sudden impact against her body like a pebble dropped from the night sky. Pain stabs the soft spot where her neck joins her skull. It flares in lightning scrawls behind her eyelids, then descends and lodges behind her rib cage.

"You are so beautiful." Perish angles her face to catch the light. "Perfect."

"No," she says. His body crests against her like a wave, and she feels the need to free herself from him, to cling to something steady in his place. Her eyes fix on a guardrail at the river's edge. Though the railing is too far away to reach, she sees it in the distance, twisted iron framing bits of water between black rectangles. Narrowing her gaze, she sends a patch of water downstream, where it floats into the sea. A million shimmering fish now released into open water. The Atlantic, where, at a point farther south, a hurricane scales its way up the coast.

Overhead the sky is clear. Her mother hovers in a starless space over land and sea, the locus between points in the night sky, the blackness between stars that call her home. *"Tadaima,"* she says to the black sky. She can see it. As clearly as she has ever seen anything, she sees her mother, and with her the knowledge that she left the home that she found after she left her mother. She is the one who left; the one who promised to stay forever has never left her. She has left the home she shared with Joseph, and she will never have a home with Perish. This certainty comes like a shadow parting the moon. It happens and is gone.

It is night, and she is alone with Perish, and the sky unfolds in waves. He looks confused, shifting his weight from his real foot to his false one. She cannot deny the truth they once knew together, but her mouth opens to speak the words that began forming long ago. "I'm not perfect," she whispers. "Don't you see that now?"

He pulls her to him, pressing her wet cheek against the hard warmth of his chest. But farther down, his metal leg feels cold and rigid between her legs and she moves her shin away so as not to be touching it. She doesn't know why she should see it differently now. She, who has always balanced effortlessly around his false leg, danced around it as if it were a living thing. The foot is wedged between hers like something dead, like the lifeless thing that it is. Her toe brushes against its hard edge, and it trips her. He tries to catch her, but her balance is already lost and she goes down.

"I'm sorry," he says, extending a hand to help her up.

"Shit," she mutters, taking his hand with one of hers and using the other to dust herself off. "Ouch."

"I'm sorry." Perish sounds irritated.

"It's okay." She turns from him and walks away from the river calling her. "I'm hungry. I don't think we've eaten all day."

She knows he cannot keep up with her. She can hear the uneven rhythm of his stride, and his displeasure quickly gives way to desperation. "You are like a bird," he says. "A beautiful bird."

"I need to eat."

"Birds need to eat twice their weight in food every day. Or else they die."

The pain comes again, a throbbing that begins this time between her ribs.

"I can't rescue you."

"Kiss me again."

He pretends not to have heard her, and she pretends not to notice. She stops once more to face him, and the urgency of his tongue inside her mouth pulls her into him like a giant hook.

Water wants to run downhill, Jessie knows. It clings to the curve of the earth, which is its natural course. Jessie tells Lily what she has learned in school, that water follows the laws of nature, which can be counted on the way she counts on Lily. But Lily does not hear *water*. She hears Jessie's voice in the sway of breeze off the East River, and in it the ridiculousness of trying to make water run uphill.

They eat in the hotel, at a table set in front of a picture window that offers a panoramic view of the city. High above the river, she spots one star and then another. She's played this game before with her children. She thinks of them tucked into their beds, the fragrance of childhood thick in their hair. *I will never betray you, never.* Because she once offered them life, doting on them and then releasing them at night to dream their dreams and create a life without her. This is the life of the mother, the life of the flower.

There is a kind of love that is youthful, the kind you do not choose, the kind that happens when you are not looking and cannot be prepared for where it will take you. It has taken Lily to New Mexico, to live in a house made of dried mud with a husband and two small children. Now it has left her off in New York. There is the love that you choose and cannot resist, and high above the river on East Thirty-eighth Street, caught between desire and fear, she can feel her heart breaking.

A clear night late in fall. A half-moon and stars like an outstretched arm pointing the way home. She sees them now. The stars. The car. The road. Ice that could not be present this early in the season, black ice that makes the car skid. Her father sees the ice. The ice that is not there shattering like a million shimmering fish released into the sea.

Y ou are what I have dreamed of all my life," Perish tells her. "You are my dream."

"I can't do this," she whispers into his closed eyes.

"No," he says. "I understand."

"What will we do?"

"Go home, I suppose."

"But didn't you think about that?"

"No, I guess I was too busy thinking about other things."

"Like what?"

"Like how badly I wanted you."

You plan as well as you can. But the past is nothing you can plan for. That's why there is a right way to do everything: it will become obvious if you think about it. You have no choice about the past. You can see it, you can keep looking back at it, but you will never change the consequences. That's why you must do things the right way. Do it the right way, or life drags behind like the weight of ten thousand dreams.

T he return ticket costs less. She does not think to ask why this is, only hands over her credit card gladly the second time around. At this hour her children will be waking. Jessie will loft into consciousness, hearing first her own breathing, and then the breathing that is not hers—so close, so safe—filling the room like a promise. She will listen to the crinkle of Misha's diaper as he rolls from his tummy onto his back, stretching his legs into the air like the crooked neck of a crane. They will listen to each other, and then to the sounds the rest of the house makes, their eyes pooling in the soft darkness before they venture down the hall hand in hand, in search of a parent. This morning they will find Yas instead. Perched on the end of his bed like some featherless parrot. Misha will see him and scream, "I don't want you, I want my mommy" while Jessie runs off to find Joseph, who will hightail it down the hall, tossing Misha into the air with tickles and declarations of love and delight. "How did you sleep?" His smile will be contagious as he nudges his nose between Misha's ribs, breathing his own scent in the damp sweat of Misha's curls. "Are you ready for breakfast?

"Come on, Jessie. You help Daddy cook, okay?"

And what will they eat? Will it be oatmeal as usual, topped with tiny cubes of butter and brown sugar? Will he remember to slice the cantaloupe ripening on the counter? If he serves it in chunks (the way he likes), the children will complain and not eat it. There will be a fight, with Joseph throwing his arms up in disgust and saying that he doesn't care whether they eat it or not. Perhaps Misha's diaper will be dry, and Joseph will remember to sit him on the potty before it's too late. Setting the knife on the cutting board, he will sweep his son into the crook of his arm like a football and dash down the hall to the bathroom, lauding him for such spectacular control. Meanwhile, Jessie, left alone in the kitchen with the knife, will take over with the cantaloupe, slicing it into long, thin smiles the way she and Misha like it. *Careful with the knife, Jessie. It's very sharp. I know you've never slipped before, but Daddy's with Misha, and I'm not there yet.*

Jessie will work in silence, the knife grazing the plastic surface of the cutting board in slow, imprecise motion, cantaloupe slipping over the edge and needing to be scooped off the floor. The irregular shapes look perfect to her as she picks off tufts of dog hair. Everything is going fine. Life goes on without the mother. Aside from Misha's one outburst, no one has even asked where she is.

It has been fewer than twenty-four hours since she left, and perhaps it is really that no time has passed at all. The door still opens when her key slides in the lock. The children are sitting around the kitchen table, the breakfast dishes not yet cleared away. They are all back at the old teak table where she first felt in her body the wavering that would later be identified as seizure, the cause of which might never be explained. It seemed inevitable then that life had started on a course that could not be halted. Except that today the sky overhead is brilliantly clear. The children are using Tempera paints to color the mountains, staring from their white typing sheets out the window through which every crag and fissure in the bony Sandias seems visible in the early autumn light. Loren presides over the artwork, producing a pen for Jessie to sign her name at the bottom.

"I'm writing *To Loren*," her daughter says proudly. "Because it's for you."

"Why, thank you very much!" Loren says with a hug and a brief smile at Lily that she cannot read.

In the split second before her presence is acknowledged, Lily notices how Loren has placed newspaper underneath the painting surfaces to ensure that stray colors will not seep through. She should thank her for this, something Joseph would never think of, but she wants to say instead that she shouldn't have bothered. Joseph purchased the table in New York the year they were married. It has stood up to years of spills and messy art projects, and that is its charm.

"Mommy!" Jessie looks up and squeals. Misha does not lift his head from his painting. "Where have you been?" Jessie demands.

Joseph stands over Misha like a sentry. He does not look up, but she can feel his ears straining for an answer.

"I had to go away."

"But you said—"

"And I missed you."

Joseph says nothing. Vacating his post behind Misha's chair, he turns his back to her and leaves the room. Jessie tells Loren that her painting is called *How the Earth Was Made with Color and Light*. Misha dabs huge swatches of color on his and says his is titled simply *Spider*. Lily moves in front of Loren to kiss her children and admire their artwork before following Joseph into their bedroom, where she pauses beside the bed just long enough to see him crouched against the headboard, a pillow crushed against his chest. She can tell from the pillow that he is showing enormous restraint. Joseph, who doesn't like to hold things in his lap, is flattening the pillow with an otherwise absent expression. Lily follows his gaze to the cherry tree outside the window. The leaves are thinning. Past the peak of their growth, they expose a stuccoed dividing wall covered with spindly vines, and beyond, a house. Privacy is illusory; what was once hidden comes closer as if overnight.

"I didn't know if you'd be back," he says. "I honestly didn't know what to tell the children. I thought you might be dead."

"Well, as you can see, I'm not dead," she says.

"Great," he says. "Why did you bother to come back?"

She shrugs. There are a number of ways to answer this question. In the tone it was given, or she could lie, but she has done enough of that.

"Maybe I don't want to know," he says.

"You don't want me to tell you—"

"I want you to think very carefully before you say anything." His hands are no longer moving. His body is perfectly still except for his eyes, which implore her to take him seriously. "I want you to know that what you say, no matter what it is, will change all of our lives. Of course our lives have already been altered by you. But you can set us back even more if you are not very careful."

"Do you want me to leave?"

"Lily," he says, clearly exasperated. "If it were up to me, yes."

"I don't want to make you unhappy," she tells him. "I don't want to be unhappy."

"I'm not sure that matters."

"Our happiness, you mean?"

"Careful—" he is saying as Misha pops into the door frame, painted from chin to fingertips in green and blue.

"Dammit. Ask Loren—" Joseph demands from his position on the bed, but Lily doesn't give him a chance to finish.

"I'll go," she offers, guiding Misha by the shoulders into the children's bathroom, where she undresses him and dunks his small body into the basin for a wash. Not bothering to remove the stray specks of color spattered across the sink and countertop, she leaves the bathroom carrying Misha peeking out from a fresh towel to find the house empty except for Jessie.

"Where is everyone?" Lily asks her daughter, but Jessie, still applying the last bit of color to her painting, merely shrugs.

"There they are." Twisting a hand free from the towel, it's Misha who points out the window for Lily to see what he sees.

Two blond heads bob in the distance. There are many walkers in the neighborhood, and from so far away these two might be anyone, except that Lily understands somehow what Misha must have sensed also. She wonders how much Misha really knows. Does he see his father and their next-door neighbor as a couple? Lily knows that Misha is fond of Loren. She'd make a great mother, Lily is sure of that; she wishes briefly that Loren's love of her children could change everything. Loren and Joseph could continue walking, turning back only for the children. Misha and Jessie would be safe with Loren. Joseph would be safe with Loren.

But even if Joseph were attracted to Loren, she doubts he would betray his wife. He understands what it means to be faithful, something she no longer understands at all.

But maybe that's not true. She has always understood about faith. There was a time when every fiber of her body depended on her mother for survival. There was faith in her gaze when her mother held her and crooned love into her ear. She carried first Jessie and then Misha inside her body as if by faith. It was faith that sealed her vow to Joseph, and a different kind of faith that destroyed it. She has always considered him the more faithful of the two of them. But maybe what he understands is really determination.

With Misha still naked and towel-wrapped in her arms, she excuses herself from Jessie to check in on her father and finds him sitting, she could swear, in the same position she'd left him in the day before. "What happened to those days when you used to wander through the house?" she asks playfully, then adds, "Not that we didn't worry about you then, but I think you'd be better off moving at least a little. No?"

He does not respond to her voice; she does not expect him to. "Let's get your sheets changed," she says, smiling.

He knows this routine well. It's always been her job. And since his arrival at the house, he's seemed to appreciate clean sheets. She's seen his body relax, curl between fresh sheets, as if he'd been invited by them to stay awhile.

"Come on!" She drops Misha's feet over the chair next to the bed in an attempt to free her arms. But Misha growls, and Yas's face tightens as if in pain.

"I'll be right back, Misha," she explains, prying his arms from around her neck. The towel falls from his shoulders, leaving him exposed, and she can see that his body is trembling. "I'll get you some clothes, too, okay? And you can watch me."

Misha looks to Yas prone on the bed, and Lily can tell that he is scared of what he sees. "Come," she says, wrapping him back up in his towel. "I'll take you with me. See how it smells bad in here? We have to clean Grandpa Yas up."

"No," Misha bellows, and Yas's face spasms again.

"Please?"

Staring from her screaming son to her wincing father, she decides to let it go. So what if her father's skin is festering and shit-caked. Let him wait awhile longer. There is no longer anything solid inside him, and his brittle emptiness glares at her. "You win," she concedes to her father and to her son. "Okay? Everyone happy?"

No one is happy, and her day, already more than twenty-four hours old, is just beginning. It's a long day, with sporadic bursts of questioning from the children punctuated by deep silences. Misha refuses to let her out of his sight. He does not want her to join in in his games of hide-and-seek and tag, but to follow along like his shadow, responding to his demands without being gratified by his usually impeccable manners. She is glad at the end of the day when the children have heard their last story. The light has been turned off. There will be no more tonight.

"Close your eyes and sleep," Lily tells them.

But Jessie's mind is still reaching for more. "Guess what I'm thinking," she pleads with Lily.

"Sleep," Lily commands.

"You have seven tries."

"If I play one round, will you promise to go to sleep right away?"

"Yes!" she cheers.

"Okay." Lily sits beside Jessie on her bed. "Just one round."

"Is it alive?"

"No." Jessie laughs. "That's one."

"Is it bigger than Daddy?"

"No." Reaching seven fingers up to her face, Jessie uses her nose to subtract two. "Only five more tries," she announces, waving one hand of fully extended fingers in the air.

"Is it a dolphin?" Misha wants to know.

"No. Dolphins are alive, and you don't get to play."

Misha starts to cry and then stops when Lily offers him one of her turns.

"Is it a shark?" Misha asks.

"No!" Jessie screams, and Lily tickles Misha's toes. "It's not even in the ocean, and now you have only three more guesses."

"Is it in the sky?" Lily asks.

"Yes. Good." Her body wiggles with excitement. "Think carefully. You're getting closer."

But Lily is completely befuddled. "Is it a cloud?"

"No! One more guess."

"A raindrop?"

"No!"

"Okay. You win. I give up."

"It's the earth, silly," she sings, giving Lily a nudge in the ribs. "You lose."

"Jessie?" Lily's voice is tentative, questioning.

"Yes. Ha-ha. You lose."

"Jessie." Lily is dubious. "The earth is bigger than Daddy."

"No, it's not."

"The earth has to be bigger than all the people who live on it together; doesn't it?"

"No. The earth is just a tiny round ball revolving around the sun. It's only this big." Jessie touches index finger to thumbtip, holding the circle against her eye like a magnifying glass. "See? You lose."

Who would dare argue? She's right, isn't she? The eye does not lie. Jessie's eye is like God's, looking down through space at the spinning mass and the multitudes. It's what she's always known.

The weeks following Lily's arrival home are frantic ones. Students needing papers returned, a missed class to schedule, the children's demands, Joseph's penetrating silence, and the phone calls, which come even though she doesn't return them, until finally Joseph appears at her office to deliver a message: the police detective has called again. Why doesn't she just call him back and do what needs to be done so she—no, everyone—can move on.

Just to be sure, he sits by the phone while she keys in the numbers scribbled on a torn strip of paper, remembering a dream she had a few nights back. A stray dog appeared on her doorstep.

It had a collar bearing faded numbers, which Joseph tried to read so she could call its owner. But he could make out the digits only one at a time, and the pauses were so long that the line kept getting disconnected.

"No, I'll come now." Lily shudders, letting the receiver clack into its cradle. "They want me to look at mug shots of sex offenders."

"Do you want me to go with you?" There is hesitancy in his voice, but also a modicum of kindness.

"No," she says, made rigid and frightened by his concern.

Perish. She has avoided him for two weeks with a lack of effort that has both surprised and exhilarated her. Now she imagines him being handcuffed and led away, pacing his prison cell like a panther. The world falling apart, the two of them together forever, though not as they would have it, locked in adjoining cells. She remembers how, not so long ago, she exonerated herself. Believed that the joy she felt in touching his flesh was simple and beyond reproach.

"We know you don't remember anything," the detective had told her. "But you are all we have to go on here." The fact is that he's right. She doesn't remember, except that she knows what is true. Words she cannot speak create a gap, and Lily exists there, surrounded by words that threaten to consume her. *Remember? I married him because I loved him; there has never been anyone else for me.*

Lily holds her breath, feeling blood surge in her head. How can this be? And shouldn't she have anticipated this moment? Her body trembles, though not for a reason she comprehends, and she stares down at her feet, at the shoes she brought out that morning, a low, wide-heeled slip-on held in place by a colorful clasp. Lily examines the leather, a muted shade of mauve. She's kept the shoes in a box at the top of her closet, waiting for them to come into style again, and this year they have. She used to own shoes like these as a child, ones with the tiny holes punched into the leather at the tip, holes in the shapes of stars that she could stare at as she walked.

At the police station, thick black books are placed on the dirty desktop in front of her. On every page, eyes stare up at her accusingly. She does not need to look. She tells herself not to look, but everywhere there is the pressure of eyes, all waiting for her to look up. She takes her time, exhibiting the paucity of a slow child—not because she cannot feel eyes everywhere, waiting for her, but because she has fallen into a gap outside of logic. She lingers just outside of time.

While a detective hovers over the desk, she wonders how long this process should take. "How are you doing?" he wants to know.

"Not good," she says. "I don't recognize any of them."

"Well, take your time," he says. "Make sure you take a good look."

Lily hears a mocking tone in the detective's voice. Shutting her eyes, she swims in the gap with words that she takes into her lungs like water so that she can expel the yes and no, the right and wrong that should be air. The detectives have wasted their time on her case; they are wasting their time even now. She could settle this mystery herself, but she takes the words into her lungs and refuses to surrender.

The detective leaves the room. She knows he has gone to meet with the detectives on the other side of the wall and that they are talking about her. They are watching through a window that opens somewhere along the cracks of the wall; their eyes are fastened on her. She wonders what horrible crimes brought men to the pages in front of her. Then, flipping through the books, she recognizes someone she's seen before. A student, perhaps? A friend of a friend? She's seen him somewhere, though she can't place where. The man at the fruit stand comes to mind. The kind, hungry-looking man who offered her fifty cents for an apple and looked so much like Perish—the man she'd vowed to pay back one day. What in his life could possibly have led him here? Her contact with him hints that she is the criminal: fifty cents, an apple, a photo. She recalls the restaurant where she sat with Perish a year earlier, the rooms that spun off one another, making it impossible to know which way faced out. The fluted wineglasses hanging upside down, their thin necks exposed, their lips casting prisms of light on the table between them. And again the hunger. The smell of the memory and the odor of the books conflate. The apple man's slack mouth is a black hole pressed against the page. She feels sick, as if the skin is lifting off her face, and she slumps to the floor.

Rushing into the room, a tall man lifts her up from the armpits and straightens her curled body into a chair. He pats at her forehead with a cold, wet towel while she sips water he's brought her from the tap. He offers her a seat beside an open window and volunteers to call her husband before sending her away. "Go home now," he says.

. . .

Joseph is cooking dinner when she walks through the door. The six o'clock news is playing softly from a portable radio he's placed on the countertop, and the children are setting the table around Yas, who is already seated.

"Hi." She circles the table to kiss each child on the cheek before greeting her father and stopping at the stove to kiss Joseph.

"Could you pour the drinks?" he asks, and she guesses nervously that he is waiting until after dinner, when the children are otherwise occupied, to talk.

Later, when the children have gone outside to play and Yas is back in his room, she goes to the couch where Joseph sits in front of the television. Having dreaded this moment, she wants it to pass with as little discomfort as possible. "So don't you want to know how it went?" she asks when a commercial comes on.

"Sure," he says, pointing the remote at the set to turn it off. "How'd it go?"

"I couldn't pick him out," she says.

"No," he says. "I thought not."

"What do you mean?" she asks, her voice rising in pitch.

"I just knew, that's all."

"But how could you have known?"

"How could you *not* have known?"

"I don't understand you, Joseph," she says bitterly. "I thought you'd be interested."

"I'm familiar with how police investigations are handled," he says with exaggerated slowness. "But I would like to know how you are. How are you?"

"I *was* feeling relieved," she says, sighing. "Before I sat down to talk with you."

He shrugs. "Sorry."

The tension mounting in the house is nearly unbearable. Her father has not come to dinner in days, and even Jessie has fallen silent. Only Misha seems unaffected, occupied by learning to buckle his sandles. Each morning for a week he shows Lily how he does it, humming "one, two, buckle my shoe" while he works. Even though it takes him longer than she can bear, he insists that she watch. She is the sun and she is the flower beneath the sun. She watches from above, the way light plays in his dark brown curls while his clumsy baby fingers grip at the leather, pushing it through the opening, then catching it on the other side. The metal clamp like a sharp tooth biting down; the tooth piercing the tongue while she watches, stiff-jawed.

"Good," she praises his efforts, except that the shoes are on the wrong feet. She watches and waits some more, in the hall on the way out the door, in the car where he likes to take off his shoes in order to repeat the process all over again.

It takes more than the ringing alarm and more than love to get her out of bed into the colder mornings and the still-dark sky. No excuses. Lunches must be ready before the children wake up.

Then they must be coaxed from dreams so that they can be fed and dressed and groomed and hurried out the door. At night Lily lies in one of the children's parallel beds, with Joseph in the other; she reads stories to Misha and catches trails of the plots Joseph creates for Jessie across the room, overhearing whispered endearments that are not intended for her ears.

Trust means believing in a future, in the existence of knowledge held by the body, and with Joseph she cannot imagine enough of a future even to do the dishes, which pile up in the sink, their contents spilling over onto the tile countertops. Misha volunteers to help, loading his plastic cups into the top rack of the dishwasher, but shattering a glass that he mistook for plastic. The dishwasher mutes the sound of Misha's cries as Joseph pulls an invisible sliver of glass from the bottom of his foot. When will it ever end?

"I can't go on this way," Joseph confesses before turning out the light.

"What way?"

"With us. Like this."

"What do you want?" Lily mumbles from her stomach, ready for sleep, ready to forget.

"I want things to be better, Lily, and I don't know how to make them better."

"I don't, either," she says, sitting up and opening her eyes to the light. She has gone off the path, no turning back. But what is wrong between them no longer has to do with Perish. When a marriage dissolves, it is never really because of a third person, she knows that. What is wrong takes place between two people, and the sad thing is that she knows she will carry it into the future if she leaves. "I know what's wrong," she says. "I just don't know how to fix anything."

"You're not just saying that?

"No."

"I don't want you to leave." He states his preference like a fact.

"I don't want to leave." It doesn't matter that she's left and returned, that she left a long time ago, and his effort to prevent what's done from ever happening might seem heroic in another circumstance.

"You're not still thinking about leaving?"

"No."

"But I can't trust you, so why should I believe what you say?"

"If you can't trust me, then why do you ask?" She doesn't mean to sound flippant, but that's the point, isn't it? She is not trustworthy, their faith is destroyed, so what difference does it make what she says? She says nothing more, but she wonders if there can be anything sadder than the failure of the heart to hold on, or the need for the heart to hold on.

She once made a promise to him, entering into a union that is sanctioned by law and speaks to all eternity, but she realizes now that marriage is daily a choice. That balmy day on the North Shore of Long Island with the flowers, so close to the ocean, trailing away like her silk dress, her tears. That day she learned about ceremony, and how the impossible can be contained in ritual because it emanates from belief. But love lasts only as long as two people want it to. And when desire ends, what then?

At night, when the children are asleep and Yas is down for the night, her conversations with Joseph continue. They keep on until one night it seems to Lily that she has nothing more to say. Lying next to Joseph, exasperated, she mumbles, "My mother hardly ever left me. Maybe that's what the problem was."

"What do you mean?" he answers, reaching over her for a book that catches his eye on the nightstand.

"I felt abandoned." She shrugs. "When she did leave, it was as if I'd died. I couldn't eat; I couldn't even move. I can remember standing at the window and listening to her heels clack as she walked down the front steps, and then I'd see her face smiling at me as my father backed the car out of the driveway. She'd wave good-bye until the car disappeared, then I'd watch the sky get dark and try to see things, like the outlines of trees and bushes, because I thought that if I could see things, she'd see things, too, and be safe. When it got very dark, the sitter would pick me up from behind, and my body would be all stiff, like I'd turned to wood. She'd carry me to my room, and I'd lie in bed completely still, trying to see in the darkness. I was sure that my seeing was all my mother had to keep her safe, so I never closed my eyes."

"I'm not sure I understand what you're talking about."

"People used to say I was an odd child, but I never worried about myself." She laughs. "And, you know, I don't think anyone else ever worried about me, either. I was the perfect child. When my mother got home, I could hear the sitter tell her how easy I'd been. 'No trouble at all,' she'd say. But of course no one had any idea the anguish I experienced, or the concentration it took me to bring my mother home safely. It was really very difficult work."

Lily imagines, as she often does, the accident that killed her mother. A windy night in late fall. No clouds, no fog or rain obscuring the road, an unbroken white line lit by a half-moon and stars. There is no logic to any of it. The car careening off the flat stretch of thruway on a clear, moonlit night. Her father was driving, and he walked away.

"You weren't an odd child," Joseph concludes aloud. "You're an odd adult."

"Yes." She smiles. "But it felt right to tell you that just now."

"Good," he says. He rises, most likely on his way to the bathroom, and she is filled with panic by this simple gesture.

"What I'm saying is that I think I understand something differently," she says, tacitly begging him to stay. "All my life I've worried about being abandoned by my mother, but maybe I was worried about the wrong thing."

Joseph hovers over the bed. "She's dead," he mutters, as if to correct an error in her logic.

She accepts his ostensible lack of engagement, knowing he's not disinterested. "For the last twelve years I've been seeing my mother standing in the entryway to the house where I grew up. I see her that way when I'm not even thinking about her. I always figured it was because she was leaving. She was getting ready to leave me. So I ignored her—because I wanted her to stay."

Joseph has made his way to the bathroom, and Lily adjusts her voice to offset the flushing toilet. "But I'm the one who left," she says. "Do you see what I'm saying?"

"No." He returns to the bed, stretches, yawns, and looks at her in the light. She can tell he's tired but trying to understand.

"I'm sorry, Joseph," she says, not quite understanding herself. "Come to bed."

"I'm exhausted," he says, turning off the light.

"Me, too." She yawns, rolling away.

"You understand some things better than just about anyone I've met," he tells her moments later in the darkness.

"What do you mean?" she asks, turning onto her back to stare up at the ceiling.

"I like your attentiveness. The way you talk about growing up, the way you care for the children."

"Thank you," she says, smiling.

"The thing I don't get," he continues, "is your complete inability to gauge the future. I used to think you were kidding—the things you couldn't see coming—but now I see that it's true."

Lying in the darkness, Lily lets her mind wander back to Perish and all that she couldn't anticipate. She thinks of her mother, tries to recall the image that's haunted her for so many years, but it's gone, and she listens instead to Joseph's breathing beside her. "I'm sorry, Joseph," she says at last.

"Everyone has their flaws, Lily," he says softly, brushing her cheek with the flat of his hand. "It's something I love about you— that maybe because you don't look ahead, you can get inside things. But just because you can't see it—." He stops, and by the silence she can tell that his heart is breaking.

"Go on," she says to him. "Please."

"We have a family, Lily. I want to see the future."

"Yes," she says. "Maybe I haven't needed to see ahead because you're so good at it."

"Thank you," he says, "I think."

"I'm exhausted," she says.

"Me, too," he confesses. "But the funny thing is, I want to make love to you."

"Okay," she says.

His hands move along her back, down her legs, form consent between them like the signature on a contract. "Is this okay, really?" he says.

Shut up, she wants to say. "Yes."

He is rough with her, and she lets him be. He jerks and spasms on top of her, whether from pleasure or acute pain she does not know. "It's not me," he swears to her before he climaxes. "It's not me."

A quarter moon appears in the middle of the day, high in the clear blue sky. Misha sees it first, which angers Jessie. Lily sees it and congratulates Misha on his good eye, but this only leads to shouts. "I saw it first."

"You didn't see it. I saw it. It's my moon."

How can such a dispute possibly be settled? Yet one more point of conflict, the world enlarging, the pulse quickening and fading.

"It's no one's moon," Lily says. "The moon belongs to the sky, not to any one of us."

Misha begins to cry. "It's my moon," he whines.

"Misha," Lily relents. "I think you're right. I think it's your moon and that it came out today just for you."

He smiles. The mother is right. The moon will be his for a day.

The flowers have begun to wilt, the leaves to drop from their branches, to spread like a new layer of skin and crackle beneath the children's shoes. The herbs must be potted and brought inside, the rhizomes dug up and divided, before it's too late. Good-bye, vine-ripened tomatoes and cucumbers. No more squash until next year. Now the backdrop of trees is brown, with a spattering of gold and orange to draw out the eye.

Brown suits the desert, but it does not suit Lily. She takes Yas with her into the garden, even though he no longer enjoys being outdoors. No longer feels safe when he is not in his room, where he finds familiarity in the four walls that embrace him like the blanket laid across his lap.

"You're safe out here," she tells him, sitting him in a lawn chair, uncoiling his rigid limbs to simulate repose. "See the leaves? Feel the breeze on your face. You're not too cold, are you?"

He smiles benignly, and she is sure he does not recognize her today.

"You know," she says, "it's been almost a year since you came to stay with us."

She accepts his silence like a reply; he has not spoken a word in days.

"Do you remember when Jessie, Misha, and I came to meet you at the airport?"

Of course he does not remember, she knows. But as she digs up the garden, she can't help talking to him as if to herself, a way to pass the time and maybe even stir his memory.

"That day was cool like this one, and sunny, remember? I watched you coming toward me, and then you walked right past me, and we had to chase you down." Chasing Yas, like chasing memory. He was once young, living in a time that linked him to her mother, the earth, her home, words that meant the whole world. Now his face is weathered from years of working in the sun, his skin soft like a baby's but slack with age. His glazed, dull eyes see nothing. That he is her father matters far less than it used to. There was a time when his praise or anger had the power to change something inside her. Now the world takes shape inside the garden, where tomatoes with wormholes the size of dimes shrivel on the vine, bugs eat the unpicked squash, and weeds grow between the furrows and must be yanked from the ground.

"Dammit," she says, plucking a thorn from her fingertip.

"Lily." She hears Yas calling her, and she stumbles out of her crouched position to go to him.

"Use gloves," she thinks she hears him say.

"Gloves?" she repeats, bending next to his ear. She is not sure she has heard him correctly, but next to hers, his face is expressionless.

She begins to cry, and her tears wet the soil, and she begins to laugh. Dirt coats her fingertips and sticks beneath her nails. He is right about the gloves. She gathers the dry brown remains of the garden into a pile and strikes a match. Flames dart into the air, sending up smoke that covers her skin and clothing with the bitter smell of fire and ash. All that has been pulled from the earth now vanishes into the sky.

Acknowledgments

Many thanks to Nancy Barickman, who got it the first time; my colleagues in the English department at the University of New Mexico, Lee Bartlett, Louis Owens, and Minrose Gwin, for their confidence in me and patient nurturing of my work; Julie Mars, Eileen Penner, Helena Brandes, and Larry Goeckel, for their insightful reading of the manuscript in various stages; Lois Kennedy and Alyson Thal-Gonzales, for insisting on my well-being; Dani Shapiro, for jump-starting the work when it seemed that all was lost; Gail Hochman, my wonderful agent, for giving me the test and allowing me to pass; Sally Kim, for her indefatigable good spirit; Kiyomi and Emiko, children extraordinaire, who pledged cooperation in the bathtub and agreed to forgo their bedtime ritual so that their mother could make last-minute changes on her manuscript; and Issa Baby of the World, big girl in training.

And always, to my husband, Jonathan Wilks, who contributed with love and much more when asked to read again and again.